CIRQUE DES FREAKS
AND OTHER TALES
OF HORROR

By the Author

Missed Connections

Cirque des Freaks and Other Tales of Horror

CIRQUE DES FREAKS AND OTHER TALES OF HORROR

by

Julian Lopez

2020

ISBN 13: 978-1-63555-689-6

This Trade Paperback Original Is Published By
Bold Strokes Books, Inc.
P.O. Box 249
Valley Falls, NY 12185

First Edition: April 2020

Credits
Editors: Jerry L. Wheeler and Allison Fradkin
Production Design: Susan Ramundo
Cover Design By Tammy Seidick

Acknowledgments

I want to acknowledge Gregg Oreo and Marshall Thornton for having read and critiqued these stories with utmost honesty.

Dedication

To my siblings for listening to my horror stories when the typewriter still served its purpose and we were all so young.

TABLE OF CONTENTS

A MASKED CAMARADERIE

Journal entry:
Venezia, Locanda Sant'Agostin
17 luglio 1932

Some mystics believe ancient cities and otherwise smaller villages serve as prisons where histories are engraved and even strangely repeated. Perhaps this had been a repeat, a distorted echo in an old city, to never again become forgotten, nor engulfed by its dark and ubiquitous waters. How could it not have ever occurred in history—a reunion, a stranger, and a conquest? But despite my orderly speculations, it has taken me more than a couple of years to revisit that place of an earlier summer and to archive the moment so, at the very least, this gruesome history may *not* repeat itself, and instead become imprisoned forever.

The year was 1929, just prior to the shattering American stock market crash. My intuition, and old college acquaintances, led me to Venice, where my investments guaranteed my security and comfort at an early age. Also, it provided an opportunity for me to focus on my writing, something I had resentfully dismissed after graduating *cum laude* from Harvard Business School. In the decade that followed, my career in commercial investment made my father and me bitter rivals. Our rivalry occurred after my management of my inherited investments did not go his way. But the discrepancy of a father's expectations for his son is irrelevant. I mention the subject as a matter of establishing the friction that also led me to Italy.

I ventured on to Venice, where I became reacquainted with Phillip; his wife, Eva; and our old Harvard friend Edward. Phillip and Edward were my fraternity brothers. Phillip had married and was living in Venice, managing the traffic of his father-in-law's exporting cargo company. According to Phillip, the highly ranked company connected Venice with other Mediterranean ports: Alexandria, Haifa, Istanbul. He had been living there for approximately seven years and had insisted on my visiting.

I knew Edward had only agreed to visit for the summer to fill his mind with Phillip, and forget the failure of yet *another* dwindling art exhibition he had diligently invested the past two years in, even though he never would have admitted to its failure. He didn't need to. Phillip's letter had clued me in to his concerns for his friend's countless futile independent gallery exhibitions, all of which Edward's family funded.

Still a bachelor, Edward lived on a cobblestone street in Greenwich Village. He managed to maintain tenuous ties with Phillip, which was about the same as I could claim. Fondly, we had shared flasks of whiskey in our dorms and recounted foolish experiences with girlfriends who, we insisted, could never disperse our brotherhood.

Well, the power of women proved otherwise. At least, such was the case for Phillip following graduation and his visit to Venice. I wasn't sure why, but I could sense some resentment from Edward when I was visiting New York and happened to cross his path at the opening opera of *The Marriage of Figaro*. I escorted Estelle, a family friend, and met Edward in the crowd. That night, I couldn't help remembering how I had always sensed an unusually intimate bond between Edward and Phillip. Something told me their brotherhood was forever, despite expansive oceans and a limiting wife.

In our exchange of letters about the reunion, Phillip told me he was excited to see me after all these years. However, I could tell he was more enthusiastic about Edward's agreement to join us than anything else. He couldn't hide it in his letter, at least not between the innuendos I deciphered so well.

All that truly mattered for me was knowing I was going to reacquaint myself with two old friends as well as rekindle the flame for my writing.

An opportunity to live in Venice had presented itself, and I couldn't deny my enthusiasm, but also, I knew the new times would be just like old times.

❖

Upon taking a small ship over the coast of Italy, sailing over the same eternal waters Venice shared, I immediately grasped how elaborate the city was, even from afar. It was ages old and yet ageless, as alluring as an individual who has captured one's heart. This place promised a different world, one where fantasy became reality through its fashions and medieval traditions, and where soirées and escorts maintained their integrity despite the imprudence permitted by more modern centuries. Monumental magic reflected in its dark waters, and even the mild scents funneled along its streets would never permit cosmopolitan complexities like automobiles to invade its ancient paths and bridges.

The second the small ship landed on the dock, I saw Phillip and Eva eagerly awaiting my arrival. Edward stood smiling at their side. I recognized his pale, ghost-like skin and parted black hair instantly. As for Phillip, a few unpleasant pounds had come with married life, but not enough to impeach his handsome physique or charming character. He was still the same Phillip, capable of being labeled a ladies' man with his deep golden-blond waves and honey-colored eyes. His smile also remained unchanged and engaging.

Both Edward and Phillip waved vigorously after spotting me and rushed over, welcoming me with hugs and a brusque patting, as if time hadn't passed between us.

Eva, an Italian beauty with white porcelain skin, large dark eyes, and a short, raven-dark bob, seemed amused at our embracing behavior.

"James! Old friend!" said Phillip, reaching for Eva's hands. "I present to you my beautiful wife, Eva!"

"I've heard so much about you," I said. "Truly, no matter how complimentary Phillip was, he could not come close to describing your beauty."

Eva curtsied and then chortled, half bashfully. "Phillip," she began in her subtle Italian accent, her slender fingers over her chest, "had I known your handsome friends were so flattering, I would have demanded they visit much sooner."

Phillip laughed, reaching for my brown leather equipage.

"No carriages?" I asked, knowing the answer even before I completed my question.

"Only if we were midgets and our horses were ponies," said Edward.

We all laughed, which reminded me how quick and witty Edward could be.

"Ah, Edward! How I have missed you," I said. "This is going to be quite a summer!"

"Boys will forever be boys," said Eva, "as you Americans like to say."

The *fondaco* building, with two lateral towers on each end, was home to Phillip and his wife, a property Eva's father gave to the young couple as a wedding present. It was a combination of Byzantine, Gothic, and Baroque architectures typical of Venice, and it overlooked Canal Grande, known by the Venetians as *Canalasso*. Its walls were the color of fresh peaches, adorned by white concrete moldings. The interior of the residence resembled an overly spacious penthouse, with classic tiles, sharply arched windows, and balconies that overlooked *Canalasso*. An opaque fresco of Etruscan influence, depicting a dancing female with castanets, stretched across the grand foyer's wall. Everything about the *fondaco* smelled of the fusion of ancient city walls and waters that funneled and lived among its citizens.

Edward and I were each given our personal room, also overlooking the *fondaco*'s adjacent dark waters.

After our Mediterranean-style dinner, prepared by a slender woman who spoke only her native language, the four of us gathered in the large living room and began recounting old academic stories and politics. We continued this way, nearly finishing a bottle of French cognac, until well after midnight.

Eva retired first for the night. I thought Phillip would be joining her, but the instant she vanished, he suggested we men continue the night with a stroll near Canal Grande. I ruminated on the reason: Edward and Phillip wanted to end up alone, eventually.

Never before had I any negative thoughts about Phillip and Edward's intimate friendship until that night. I knew it was because of Eva. I don't know why, but I had immediately become very fond of her. Perhaps it was Eva's elegance and congenial personality, a set of virtues I rarely encountered in American women.

That night, I remained pasted to my comrades' sides as we aimlessly wandered through the night. Along the still waters, however, I, too, grew tired and departed, leaving Edward and Phillip on their own.

❖

After a brunch on Toledo the next morning, the four of us basked in the sun over the still waters, sharing a gondola and even a bottle of champagne. Eva informed us of an annual ball near Basilica di S. Marco she wanted us to attend.

"We will all need masks!" said Edward. "Even you two scoundrels! *Especially!*"

Eva squinted, opening her silk umbrella to shield her from the sun. "You need not worry, dear Edward. I have the perfect eye masks for all of us."

"Oh, yeah..." Phillip added, half smiling. "She's been raving about these old masks she discovered in a secret compartment in the basement of our home."

"Yes," said Eva. "And I have been wanting to make use of them. I don't know why anyone would have stashed them away! They're really old, perhaps centuries. Plus, they're quite elegant and very well-made."

"How exciting," said Edward. "I'm the kind of boy who never turns down a decadent soirée."

"How many masks did you find?" I asked.

Eva smiled, her left eyebrow rising exquisitely. "Four."

❖

That late evening, as the sky intensified its shade of blue into one blatantly dark and permissive of auras, such as the ones that surrounded the stars and the svelte moon that smiled on a warm Venice below, we arrived at the elaborate ball.

Indeed, Eva had been correct about the Venetian eye masks. Everything about their intricate detail and vibrant colors with gold trimmings was too beautiful to have been stashed away. Their papier-mâché and silk ribbons were in mint condition. And although we could not pinpoint the masks' exact age, they certainly seemed centuries old.

Everything about the decadent ball reflected the allure of Venice, one that continues to hold true today, like a world separate from the rest of its country.

Elaborate gowns, coifs, and men's silk suits of pearl-white over white stockings seemed like an afterthought to the array of feathered and bejeweled masks, some resembling mystical characters. Laughter, dancing, and endless trays of champagne circled the large hall and its coliseum interior of several floors, each atop large marble pillars.

Eva and Edward danced together for a long part of the night, until Phillip intervened, closing in on his wife and planting a kiss on her without removing his mask. Eva stretched her lips widely.

"It's like kissing a stranger," she told her husband, before tossing her head back and gaily laughing.

"Very funny," said Phillip. "I could easily say the same, being that none of us have removed our masks."

"Why would anyone want to show their true identity?" Edward snarled. He seemed to be having difficulty focusing on Phillip and Eva, revealing just how much champagne he had consumed.

"Hey, how about something to eat?" I spoke to Edward suddenly, attempting to divert the intense gaze he gave the couple—Phillip in particular.

"I'm fine," he said, partially slurring his words. When I reached for his wrist, he pulled away defensively.

Both Phillip and Eva looked over at Edward.

"Are you okay?" asked Eva.

"I think you may have had enough, Edward," said Phillip.

Edward smirked, allowing a mild laugh to escape his lips.

"I think it's the atmosphere and the champagne," I said. "We've *all* had plenty tonight."

"Well, isn't that what masking our faces is all about?" Edward remarked, more a statement than a question. His eyes never left Phillip. "After all, what's the point of wearing these if one has to behave?"

Before anyone could answer, Edward squeezed through the stirring crowd, disappearing in its thickness.

I ambled slowly behind, but not to follow Edward. Instead, I picked up a glass of champagne from a passing tray, in full agreement with Edward's remark about the masks. He had been right. All night it had partially and glamorously covered my face. And, just like always, I remained aloof to all the mischievous actions around me—masked or unmasked—without partaking.

Almost desperately, I emptied the glass with a brisk swig.

That was when the gentleman startled me with his words. He stood tall in white silks. The slick waves and shine of his blond hair reflected impeccably under the light.

"They say a man should always drink slowly," he said. "It keeps him mysteriously intriguing."

I looked over, discovering an ebony eye mask with short, raven-black feathers along the sides of its almond-shaped eyeholes. Its wearer had the most intense green eyes. They pierced me.

"Really?" I asked, presenting my best witty smile. "Even when aiming for utter intoxication?"

He smiled below the sheer silver trimming outlining his black mask. Several miniature black rhinestones above its left eyehole gleamed over the silk finish of the eye mask, further enhancing its chic sense of elegance.

"Especially when aiming for utter intoxication," he said in a crisp, soothing tone. A set of flawless white and perfectly aligned teeth shone behind his lips. His nose was as admirably sculpted as his chin. His shoulders were broad, slanting slightly under his Victorian-fringed silk shirt. A golden vest with a dark paisley pattern matched his solid silk Capris. The tight pants revealed the muscles in his thighs and, when he turned, so did the enticing dimples along the sides of his powerfully muscular *derrière*. Also, his ample calves were defined nicely beneath his white silk stockings.

Slowly he raised his hand, opening it flatly before me. An emerald pinky ring sparkled almost too intensely. "Marcello. At your service."

"James," I said, as I took his soft, warm palm. He clasped my hand and brought it slowly to his lips. The smack was audible and aroused my attention.

Again, I found myself gazing into his fascinating green eyes. I had never before known such intensity, not even with Estelle, whose heart I had attempted to please many years earlier. He rested his thumb under my chin, which he raised gradually so my eyes would lock with his. Though masked, we were bold and unconcealed—brown and green eyes aiming in one direction.

He leaned forward and whispered in my ear, "Come with me."

I nodded, recognizing the internal fervor that rushes down one's body when in a frenzy and consumed with passion. Just as I was about to bid the soirée adieu, I heard familiar voices calling my name.

It was Eva and Phillip, holding hands and their champagne.

"Who's your friend?" Eva cooed. Her large eyes moved back and forth behind her red and gold mask.

"This is Marcello."

"Have you seen Edward?" asked Phillip.

"No. I can't imagine where he went."

"Oh, there he is!" Eva exclaimed, raising both hands. "Edward! Edward, honey!"

Distantly, Edward watched us all. He held an open bottle of champagne, as if no longer content to consume the fizz under the limited proportions of a stingy slender glass. To my surprise, Edward gazed at me with a certain seriousness that made me uncomfortable. He didn't even stop looking at me as he approached, or when he reached us.

"So, who is your new friend? I've been watching you acquaint yourself with him from afar," Edward said, his smile forming mostly on the right side of his face. "I can read lips, you know. *His* lips."

Marcello faced Edward and smiled. "Funny the stories one fabricates when assuming across a room without knowing. You see, Edward, it is *I* who am desperately aiming to acquaint myself with James." His eyes widened as his smile disappeared. "Do you still read lips?"

Edward began to laugh, adjusting the mask—purple with hints of lamé—over his face. "Oh, dear friend, you are quite an amusing *bambino*."

"Oh, Edward," Eva said, "don't be condescending. Marcello is quite a gentleman, and I think it's marvelous James has befriended such a charming *chevalier!*" Her eyes fixed on Phillip. "Don't you, honey?"

Phillip shrugged as he pressed his lips together, synchronizing with the direction his shoulders had dropped. "I don't know. I think it is fine, so long as he and Marcello find some great Italian dames at this ball to accompany them. Isn't that right, Marcello?"

Uncertain how to interpret Phillip's suggestion, I looked at Marcello, then at Edward.

Edward laughed once again and nodded, only this time with a bitterness I had never detected before.

"Actually, Phillip is completely right," he said, before guzzling vulgarly from the bottle.

We all watched silently until he spoke again.

"I will do the same. I will find me a great Italian dame—not as beautiful as you, Eva. Clearly, you are magnificent. But I will find one and make her mine. She will be mine, and I will be hers...tonight."

Phillip tried to snatch the bottle away from Edward, but couldn't reach it. "You're goddam drunk, Edward!" he cried.

"And you, dear old friend, shouldn't care." Edward leaned forward, his eyes sullen, as he pressed his finger on Phillip's tuxedo shirt. "You already have someone. James and I, on the other hand, are alone. We need any incentive we can find to stay true to ourselves and have the courage to follow that path, even if it means not finding someone and ending up alone forever."

We all watched in shock, attempting to make sense of Edward's words. But before any of us could respond, Edward flung the bottle against a wide pillar, shattering the hunter green into countless pieces. He shoved his way through the crowd, losing himself in the midst of its elaborate costumes, silks, and masks of porcelain, leather, and papier-mâché.

All of us watched without responding, except for Phillip, who hissed under his breath before cursing and storming off in the opposite direction.

Eva looked at us and shrugged, as if she could neither grasp nor give reason for the incomprehensible anger displayed by both men.

"Are you okay?" I asked, reaching for her hand.

"I'll be fine. I just need to calm Phillip down."

I nodded, watching her wind through the crowd as she attempted to find her husband. And just as I realized Marcello was still there, I felt the grip of his hand on my wrist.

"Don't worry about anyone at this moment. Finally we are alone, perhaps not for the entire night, so we should enjoy it. Alone."

"I feel strange leaving them all here."

Marcello smiled. "Don't be. I'll make sure we don't lose sight of them tonight."

❖

I wasn't sure if it was my attraction to Marcello or the sudden opportunity to escape the sexually tense quarrel among friends, but I allowed him to lead me away from the ball. We gazed intently at one another from behind our masks as we glided toward a different room with long, curved stairs. We climbed them and entered the upper coliseum levels, where I could see the crowd becoming smaller, its echoes decreasing with every step and disappearing when we reached the utmost balcony floor. We faced the hallway and the multiple doors along it.

"Where are we going?"

Marcello didn't answer. Instead, he rested his index finger gently over my lips, requesting my silence.

We entered the chamber at the end of the hall, finding a highly bolstered bed piled with silk spreads and a matching duvet. I saw our reflections in an elaborate wall mirror, lit from hanging chandeliers and wall sconces. A highly arched window opposite invited the dark night, a silver moon, and mostly Venetian rooftops to bear witness to the privacy between two masked men.

I looked up at Marcello, who closed the door behind us and smiled.

Without looking away, I began to reach for the ribbons behind my head to remove my mask.

"Wait," Marcello said. "I like the mystery…at least, for a little longer."

I focused on his intense green eyes. Already venturing into new territory with a gentleman, one who remained as enigmatic as any lady I had ever known, I found his request enchanting. And so I allowed myself, for the first time ever, to savor such role-playing, even as he leaned in so that our masks touched—and our lips.

Half forcefully, he clutched my hair, tugging it so that my lips widened on instinct. He dared to thrust his tongue within, savoring every bit of my mouth. At the same time, he fastened his right hand over my buttocks, pulling me against the silks that dramatically defined his broad chest and thighs. Our chests and groins rubbed together, even as all our muscles swelled and heaved, hardening in the midst of their frenzied circumstance.

We kissed savagely, our hands wrapped around each other's backs. He coiled one of his hands around my waist. But I saw him in the wall mirror, attempting to pull something out of his vest with his other hand. At first I thought the mirror was deceiving me, but even before I could render full sense of the small, sharp blade I saw in his grip, my blood turned cold. My legs became a set of severed stilts, without strength, threatening to hinder my balance. I instantly weakened and found myself pulling back, as Marcello raised the stiletto.

I reached for his wrist and he cuffed me with a harsh blow to the side of my face. During this brutal and cumbersome brawl, the silk ribbons of my mask became loose and it fell to the floor.

I looked up, alarmed, and prepared to feel the sharp and perilous blade, but Marcello was nowhere to be seen!

I looked around, fearing to discover him and his blade lurking behind me. How had I provoked him? But it was as if the chamber's air had consumed him fully, or he had vanished in the night.

My chest heaved, but this time it was for more air, not from the uncontainable sensual passion for Marcello. Either way, I headed for the door, desperately attempting to escape the chamber. But then I stopped, my hand resting on the doorknob. That's when I knew! But how could it possibly be? I hadn't been the only one who had seen him. Eva, Phillip, and Edward had also seen Marcello.

I knelt down, picking up my eye mask. I reversed it so it watched me blankly with unfilled eyes and sharp nose.

I wasn't certain why I tried it again. Perhaps it was to debunk my sudden assumption that a mask could conjure the presence of a man. But before I knew it, I had brought the mask to my face and once again aligned its peepholes over my eyes. To my horror, Marcello stood in front of me, attempting to spear me with the blade. I tossed away the mask, and he disappeared once again.

I looked up at the lonely chamber, my reflection the only one in the mirror. Even though I was fairly certain Marcello could not injure me so long as I did not wear the eye mask, a chill rushed through me, knowing he was somewhere in that room, undoubtedly invisible. Still, he could no longer harm me. I contemplated these random thoughts until I suddenly thought of another dreadful reality: Eva, Edward, and Phillip all had the same masks and were all in peril.

I grabbed the mask and stormed out of the room, nearly stumbling several times as I scurried down the spiral stairs to the main floor, where the ball continued despite the late hour.

Wondering whether the three of them were even still at the soirée, I placed the eye mask over my face momentarily and spotted Marcello in the crowd, departing the large hall through its main entrance.

Rushing out into the plaza that intersected with Basilica di S. Marco, I shouted their names and darted in the direction of Eva and Phillip's home.

All around me, darkness hindered my view and I floundered and collided with the narrow corridors and avenues that separated the ancient buildings and dwellings. The scent of the canals zoomed vigorously through my nostrils as I attempted to retrace my steps, which I foolishly could not recall.

Everything about the city seemed familiar, yet I could not remember the way to the *fondaco* until I reached the Canal Grande. I was a bit disoriented, but I also knew it would eventually stream its way against Eva and Phillip's *fondaco*. I walked next to it, at times following it behind waterfront buildings.

Before I knew it, I had reached the familiar path only yards away from their home. I saw a lucent white glow, a lump that shimmered in the narrow alley that led to their main entrance. But as I paced toward it, my heart jolted with the unbearable reality of what had collapsed there! Eva lay dead, sprawled across the brick path. Her white silk dress was covered with bloodstains from a gash in her neck.

I knew she had been ravaged by Marcello's blade.

I gasped for air as I bent down, whispering her name tearfully. She had never removed her mask.

Storming through the tall arched gothic doors of the *fondaco* past the foyer, I shouted for Phillip and Edward. Many of the lights to the *fondaco* were lit, including the upstairs, which led me to the grand master chamber. And this time, despite Eva's bloody display, I was somehow prepared to bear it.

Phillip and Edward's corpses lay naked over the bed, their bodies intertwined and incompletely concealed in the sheets, as if the interruption of their intimacy had been just as abrupt as their deaths. Their necks had been slashed like Eva's neck, and by the same madman—Marcello. Over their partially visible faces were their masks, still attached.

Journal entry:
Venezia, Locanda Sant'Agostin
24 settembre 1939

I am back in Venice, no longer within the cold walls of the *fondaco* I once dwelled in briefly among friends, but in a small cottage just east of the ancient structure.

Outside, the canals, under the moonlight, continue to flow earnestly and with the same mild seawater scent.

A decade has passed, and I am finally prepared to resume my plan and prevent history from repeating itself. I have the mask I saved with me after I tossed the other three into Canal Grande that dark, treacherous night. I feel his presence already, traveling with the wind, but I won't know for sure until I place the old mask over my eyes. Marcello will return, perhaps with his blade.

And this time, I will present him with mine.

THE MARIACHI'S SERENADE

Tradition was the last thing Adrian needed. Especially for a week in Guadalajara, the city he and Tristan had left Puerto Vallarta for. They had crammed the mighty western *ciudad* into their vacation agenda after Adrian's grandmother Elena convinced him—with *abuelita* guilt—that a visit was long overdue.

"Adrian, *mijo. ¿Como estas?*" Elena's piercing dark eyes and salt-and-pepper hair were both neutralized by her brown skin. "And who is this handsome man with you?" she asked, admiring Adrian's companion, who stood tall and bronzed, hints of red still surfacing above his cheekbones and nose.

"This is Tristan, Grandma. He's my boyfriend."

"*Hola, señora* Elena. It's definitely a pleasure to make your acquaintance. Adrian has told me all about you," said Tristan, reaching for Elena's hand. She ignored it and crushed him in an abrupt hug, planting a doting kiss on his ruddy cheek.

"*Hola*, handsome man. Welcome to my *casa*. You remind me of a boyfriend I once had when I lived in Texas as a young *chica*. Boy, was he *guapo*."

"Really?" Tristan smiled. "Adrian never told me that. Did you know this, Adrian?"

"*Mijo*, this man is a keeper," Elena said. "I can feel it, just like when your mother met your father. I knew then he would be a great man. Unfortunately, I did not know he would take her so very far away from me, raising his *familia* in Texas, that *condenado*!" Elena smiled, pumping a fist in the air. "But it's for the best. Look at you. You look great, a grown man. The last time you came to visit, you were only a teenager with hair much too long for such a handsome face."

"That's not true, Grandma. My mother and I were here just five years ago. Besides, you can always visit us, like you used to."

"Oh, Adrian. My old bones won't allow that."

"Auudrey…ahn," Tristan repeated, attempting to say his boyfriend's name with the same Latin tone Elena sang when she spoke. "I've never heard anyone call you this way, not even your parents. I like it."

"Ha ha, very funny," said Adrian. He examined the spacious two-story home. Not much had changed about it. White tile floor lay everywhere, including the curved stairs that led to the second story. Oversized floral sofas and antique furniture clashed with her arrangement of colorful clown porcelain figurines and potted plants, whose leaves she probably still varnished with mayonnaise.

"You shouldn't be ashamed." Elena frowned. "It was your great uncle's name. Adriano was your grandfather's youngest brother, may he rest in peace, *que en paz descanse*, accompanying your grandfather. Well, it was always Adriano, originally."

Adrian's eyebrows rose. "I didn't know grandpa had a brother."

"Of course he did. Your *abuelito* just didn't like to talk about it. His brother Adriano died much too young. He was about your age. A handsome fellow, just like you, my *mijo*."

"That's for sure," said Tristan, casually wrapping his arm around Adrian's waist before sliding it off, abruptly and apologetically. "Oops, sorry about the public display."

"Oh, *mijo*, you don't have to worry about showing your love to each other in front of me, okay? I love my Adrian without judgment. All our family does, as you may have noticed."

Tristan smiled. "It's great you think that way."

"Why wouldn't I? All our family accepts and loves Adrian regardless. If only my husband's parents would have accepted their Adriano without judgment, perhaps he would still be alive today."

"Are you serious?" Tristan asked. "What happened?"

"Well, it was about the same time I met Adrian's grandfather. I don't know too much, since my husband didn't like to talk about his brother. All I can remember really was Adriano was sort of shy, but such a gentleman! He didn't have a girlfriend. I guess that would have been okay, but his parents did not like the idea he wasn't interested in any of the local girls who were just crazy over him. There were rumors he had a male companion, whom his parents disliked so much, they secretly paid him a hefty sum to leave Guadalajara. Well, Adriano came home late one night so depressed. It turns out his companion went to America, leaving him and all the local gossip behind. He wanted nothing to do with Adriano."

"The nerve of my great-grandparents," Adrian bristled, "looking so benevolent in those pictures. Who would have known?"

"Exactly," Elena said. "Well, Adriano fled, claiming he was tired of the life here. He was going to the USA to find his companion. But poor Adriano's destiny wasn't written that way."

"Why's that?" Tristan asked, joining Adrian on the sofa.

Elena remained still for what seemed like an eternity before finally speaking. "The bus he took never made it. It crashed and rolled down the *carretera*."

"Wow."

"That's harsh," Tristan added.

Elena nodded. "As if that wasn't enough, Adriano's companion came back, pounding on this very door to return the money and to take Adriano with him, but it was too late. The news of Adriano's death devastated him so much, he poisoned himself. My husband and his parents were simply grief stricken. But they never mentioned another word about the companion, as if he never existed."

"The drama," said Adrian. "How Romeo and Juliet of them."

"Tell me about it," Tristan quipped. "Certainly romantic."

❖

Later that afternoon, the three of them visited the downtown area, known as *el centro*. Their sightseeing and shopping jaunt occurred in Plaza Tapatia, where the historic *Catedral Metropolitana* stood proud since 1561 with its Gothic, Baroque Moorish, and Neoclassical influence. The cathedral was the oldest of the monuments in the plaza, where other historical landmarks, including a theatre, government facilities, and a museum, all embodied the classic Spanish architecture of opaque but fascinating gray. After visiting the cathedral, Adrian wanted nothing more than to rest for the day.

As if the walking hadn't been enough for Adrian, who had lost count of how many times he had been to the *centro*, Tristan and his grandmother had expanded their itinerary. A priest named Padre Salvador, whom Elena knew personally, granted the three a private tour behind *Catedral Metropolitana*, where the toll of the bell clanged loudly and deafened Adrian. But it wasn't long before the three of them retired to a restaurant in Plaza Andares amidst affluent shoppers and trendy boutiques.

❖

By the time they returned to Elena's home, they were ready to surrender for the day. After watching a black-and-white film on television, Tristan and Adrian kissed Elena good night and headed upstairs to the guest room.

The combination of the draining sun and too much walking prompted Adrian into a deep sleep. Late into the night, Tristan grunted and awakened him. Adrian looked up at the dark ceiling, then the open window facing the main street and city below. He remained still, wondering how many times his mother, as a young girl, had looked up, eyeing the very same ceiling of her bedroom.

He was thinking about his trip when something distantly echoed into their room. It was the faint resonance of a guitar playing a gentle tune that sounded more like a lover's private whisper. Slowly, Adrian realized the music was coming directly from below his window.

He pulled the sheets away, wondering if he should wake Tristan up, but the gentle sound of the romantic tune was so soothing, he wanted to enjoy its rhythmic flow without the sudden interruption of Tristan's startled voice.

Someone was serenading his love, playing a classic *bolero* to proclaim his feelings for a specific *senorita* within one of the adjacent homes in the middle of the night.

Adrian stood up and walked toward the open window. Distant flickers of lights from the stretch of the city and the labyrinth of streets came into view through the panoramic window.

Adrian looked down at the deserted street in search of the person with the guitar but found it difficult to distinguish any musician, especially when the music abruptly stopped. All he saw were rows of boxy houses stacked alongside one another, aligning evenly. Occasionally, a small tree shaded the sidewalk, as if yearning to survive in a metropolitan city where slabs of concrete and ribbons of asphalt crisscrossed.

The *bolero* began again, gently, under one of the trees.

Adrian leaned farther out the open window until he was looking directly downward at the first-story entrance to his grandmother's house and a man approaching her door from under the tree.

Although the moon provided only vague light, Adrian could see the man was tall and wore a black outfit with thick gold threading embellishing the legs and arms. It was a traditional mariachi uniform. The mariachi, whose attention was solely focused on Elena's front door, did not wear the hat, an element that would have completed his garb. Adrian smiled, wondering why this lovelorn man was at his grandmother's house. Could his grandmother have an admirer? At her age? Countless questions ran through Adrian's mind. Before he knew it, the mariachi was looking directly up at him.

Adrian froze, watching the mariachi smile as he continued to play his guitar.

Clearly the man was serenading someone, and without any care that Adrian was watching. Adrian was about to wake Tristan, and show him something so Tapatío and traditional, when the man's smile stretched farther, handsomely creasing his upper lip. The nearby golden glow from the streetlight revealed just how truly attractive the mariachi was.

Adrian remained still, observing the mariachi's black raven hair and light skin, which could have been considered ghostly if observed too quickly and under the very same light. As for the *bolero*, the mariachi continued to play it gently, his eyes aimed at Adrian.

The singer's dark, slick hair and slight sideburns appeared clean, and even vintage, as if the mariachi had somehow escaped from a classic film featuring Pedro Infante or María Félix.

Adrian found it difficult to peel his eyes from such a cliché: a traditional troubadour who was evidently successful in enamoring any listener he could seduce.

For the first time in Adrian's life, music tugged at his heart. He could not resist such men who proclaimed themselves boldly at courtship—successful or unsuccessful—soothing human hearts the way only angelic-voiced *hombres* knew how to soothe.

Even though the serenade was not meant for him, he found himself pretending it was. That's when Adrian understood the unlimited extent and reality of his passion for his roots, specifically the custom of serenading. In this instance, however, Adrian had not found his culture; his culture had found him—through the handsome eyes of a stranger, proving his love-theory wrong. That same balladeer gripped Adrian and his heart, intriguing both with only guitar chords.

Before Adrian could decide whether he should wake his grandmother or Tristan, or even simply ignore the guy and return to bed, the mariachi began to walk away. His departure saddened Adrian.

Then the mariachi stopped walking and turned around, gesturing for Adrian to follow.

Adrian's body stiffened, and his heart skipped a beat. Uncertain how to react, Adrian watched the stranger walk down the street until he reached the corner and turned around once more. The mariachi looked up and smiled, again gesturing to Adrian to follow. Before Adrian could do anything, the man disappeared by pacing left on the corner of the street. The music faded with him, until only the silence of what *ciudad* life echoes when asleep resurfaced.

❖

The scent of world cities at daytime is always different than that of night. However, in Guadalajara, the distinction was more evident to Adrian. Centuries of history permitted its two different scents to exude vigorously—both influenced by not only the heat of day and its impassive dark sky of night, but by the smog and disproportionate rhythm to which the wind and people zoomed past.

And now, the two scents had a precise meaning for Adrian: one for adhering to the daytime pace, and the other for when only the stars bore witness. When the scent of night filtered the air, so did memories of the mariachi. They came to him like dreams, threatening once again with the same emotional ammunition from the night before, as dreams are known to do.

This time, the images of his dark hair and music—one slick, the other enthralling—had become all he could think about. The mariachi had invaded his mind.

❖

Adrian called it a night with Tristan at his side, hoping the same harmonic tunes would again interrupt his sleep. He tossed and turned, warm and cool air intermingling through the open window. But the air wasn't the only thing wafting. With the soothing wind returned the tunes of the mariachi, embracing Adrian's core. It arrived with the clockwork precision of some celestial coincidence, awakening and inviting only Adrian.

He darted toward the window. To his delight, the handsome mariachi stood outside, looking up at Adrian. Again, his lips parted and he smiled. Again, the mariachi gestured for Adrian to follow.

Adrian looked behind at Tristan, who slept soundly, his naked legs stretching open and entangling with the sheets. Adrian's heart beat with frantic exhilaration. Looking down once more at the mariachi, Adrian boldly smiled and nodded.

When Adrian stepped out into the quiet night after throwing on whatever clothes he could find, the mariachi was already heading for the corner. Adrian sprinted after him. The mariachi reached the corner and turned, facing him eye-to-eye. Adrian was stunned by his incredibly handsome smile and brown eyes.

"Hi," said Adrian. "I mean, ¿*Hola...hablas ingles*?"

"Yes," the mariachi responded, his thickly accented voice deep. "What is your name, please?"

"I'm Adrian."

"Adriano?"

"No, it's Adrian. No 'o'." Adrian smiled, leaning against the building. "This is really weird, but why are you in front of my grandmother's house? And who are you serenading?"

"You."

"Me?" Adrian's eyes widened. "Oh, c'mon, you don't even know me. If you ask me, I think you're just cruising with your guitar, knowing your beautiful music is capable of enamoring some strange fellow or *chica*."

"That is true." The mariachi smiled. "Tell me, has it worked?"

"So far it has."

"That's good to hear."

"What is your name?"

"Mauricio," he said softly but proudly as he plucked a chord on his guitar.

"You're a very handsome man, Mauricio. But aren't you worried about parading your guitar and beautiful tunes all by yourself so late at night?"

"The night is my world. How about you allow me to show it to you?"

"This is so corny," said Adrian, half laughing. "But I love it. As for that *bolero* you were playing, it's so beautiful. What's it called?"

"It's called *Historia de un Amor*."

"Aha, how appropriate. I've never heard anything like it. It truly is enchanting."

"Would you like me to play it for you again?"

"Actually, that would be great."

"Your desire, then, is my desire." The mariachi nodded. "But not here. Follow me."

❖

Perhaps it had been the golden aura of the Victorian lamp poles throughout Plaza Tapatia, or the way the cobblestone and brick colonial streets and monuments surrounding *Catedral Metropolitana* reflected, or that the *ciudad* was desolate, belonging only to this sprawling citadel, but the night had become delightful.

Adrian, who shared everything from his estranged feelings and passion for Guadalajara, to his life with Tristan, felt as if he were in a dream, one with a handsome stranger whose outfit and music served as the epitome of the city's history and flavor.

"So, I feel as though I'm doing all the talking," said Adrian, spotting a bench in the middle of the plaza, where they sat down. "Tell me something about yourself. Do you play music for a living? Are you married, single, in love?"

"Do you want me to be married?"

Adrian let out a small laugh. "I want you to tell me something true about yourself."

Mauricio looked down, bending his knees over the bench so that his guitar balanced near his thigh. "Okay, the song will say it all."

Before Adrian could say anything, the mariachi began playing the same exquisite tune, but this time he sang along, whispering words of a love not granted.

Adrian could feel his heart throbbing. As if the guitar's mellow, dramatic notes were not touching enough, the clear, rich sound of Mauricio's voice resonated with mesmeric romance, unlike anything Adrian had ever heard. His gentle, masculine echo penetrated the narrow alleys and streets of the plaza, where all noise retired and descended into the night. It spiraled to the sky, where the stars and the endless dark surrounding them met to infinitely seal all secrets.

When Mauricio completed his song, Adrian remained speechless, his face expressionless. At least, that was how he imagined himself appearing. Mauricio leaned forward, easing his lips against Adrian's, pressing gently until they parted wider, allowing his tongue to taste more of Adrian, to entice Adrian to succumb entirely.

The two men kissed, eyes closed and faces touching.

Adrian was helpless, swimming in a sea of delight and delirium. He could feel Mauricio press his hand against the side of Adrian's face and lead its way down until it stopped at his galloping heart.

"I must go," Mauricio said almost too abruptly. "The sun will be out soon."

"Wait!" Adrian's eyes focused desperately in the dim light. "How will I see you again? When? Please, when?"

"My music will call you."

Adrian nodded, unconvinced and half annoyed. "What if you accidentally wake up someone other than just me when you come back? I can't just go out and see you. Besides, I'm only here a couple more days. I would like to see you sooner."

At first, the mariachi didn't respond. He seemed to be processing the hopeful and love-lost lyrics he had just sung. It was as if the song was virtually all that the mariachi could focus on. Slowly, he kissed Adrian once more before responding. "The next time you hear me play, I want you to come with me forever."

Adrian remained silent. He knew such a request was unfathomable. Living forever in a *ciudad* that was no longer a part of him was insane. However, the mere idea of an invitation by someone so romantically hopeful and handsome brought a smile to his face.

Adrian watched the mariachi step back and wave as he began disappearing within the plaza.

"*Buenas noches.*"

❖

The next morning, at the *Mercado*, where Elena and Adrian purchased several fresh items for Elena to prepare her *chile relleno* for dinner, Adrian could not think of anything other than the mariachi.

"*Mijo*, where is Tristan?" Elena asked.

"I don't know, *abuelita*," Adrian said, thinking how much the *Mercado* easily resembled a farmer's market back home, except it fell slightly short of the sanitary restrictions. "Actually, I do know. He said he was going to some local gym near Universidad Autonoma."

"I'm surprised you didn't go with him. Shopping at the Mercado with the smell of raw pig's head and *tripas* has never been to your liking. Are you okay, *mijo*?"

"Of course. I'm fine, *abuelita*."

There was no need to disclose what was really tugging at his heart. That is, until he recognized the tune of a song achingly familiar to his heart playing on a vendor's small radio. Adrian stepped closer to make sure he wasn't hallucinating the old song that spilled from the small black speaker with hints of AM static. He focused his eyes on the small radio and his heart on the night before.

"What is it, Adrian?" Elena asked.

"This song—I know it."

"Of course, *mijo*." Elena dismissed his epiphany by nodding and smiling. "It's an old classic. Everyone knows it."

"That's not what I mean. I've been hearing this song at night. Some man has been strumming it on his guitar outside your front door."

"A man?"

"Yes, *abuelita*. A mariachi has been playing *this* song on his guitar outside your door for at least three nights. You haven't heard him?"

"Adrian, you *must* ignore him," Elena said desperately and almost too harshly.

"What? Are you serious? Who is this man?"

"I can't believe he has come back." Elena appeared flushed. She averted her gaze.

"Who is he? Tell me who this man is."

"Adrian, I don't want you to go to him or even acknowledge his existence."

"Tell me who he is, *abuelita*!"

"His name is Mauricio. He was the companion of your late uncle Adriano. He died many years ago and keeps returning, thinking Adriano is still alive. He serenades Adriano with this exact song. He hasn't appeared in many years, even before your mother was a child. I don't know why he has returned or what he wants, but you must ignore him, Adrian."

"*Abuelita*, that's insane. It can't be him."

"Sometimes he would call Adriano's name, announcing his arrival and waiting to take him away forever. This is why you must *not* go outside, Adrian! Promise me you won't."

At first, Adrian felt his blood turn cold and his knees weaken. How could he have been talking to a ghost? Better yet, how had a ghost enraptured Adrian? The two had even kissed.

Based on the panic in his grandmother's voice, he found it best to not disclose his experience. He knew he couldn't share with her his intimacies with Mauricio. Although he believed his grandmother, her story seemed all the more genuine to him when the two arrived home and Elena pulled out an old sepia-toned photograph of Adriano with his lover Mauricio next to him. Indeed, it was the *same* Mauricio with the handsome features and pale, ghostly face.

As he examined the photograph, a chill ran through Adrian's blood and even his heart, cooling any warmth or romance for the mariachi.

Adrian couldn't believe what he had experienced. He thought about it fearfully the entire night, hoping this time he wouldn't hear the beautiful guitar music. Having Tristan at his side gave him a sense of comfort. Even so, Adrian could not sleep for hours, beset by thoughts that he heard the music, even dreaming that the music echoed up to his window and the mariachi was outside.

But he *wasn't* dreaming.

Distantly, the tune beckoned and awoke him again. The mariachi was outside, and this time, Adrian knew he was waiting to take him forever. Adrian's heart raced frantically.

Romance had turned to fear, and suddenly Adrian knew he could never run away with the mariachi. He no longer wanted to hear the music. All he wanted was for Mauricio to leave. The calling guitar seemed to get louder, as if closing in on him.

Adrian could feel his body drip with cold sweat as the *bolero* echoed. Adrian wanted to scream. To tell Mauricio to stop and go away. He even thought of waking Tristan, but the music suddenly stopped.

Adrian remained bug-eyed under the sheets, his body and neck stiff without movement. He remained still for several minutes until he was sure the music had completely stopped.

He turned slowly, reaching for Tristan, something familiar and real. But Adrian felt only the sheets. Tristan was not at his side. Adrian sat up and pulled the sheets away before rushing for the light switch.

To his astonishment, Tristan was nowhere to be seen.

At the same time, Elena stormed into the room, as if she, too, had heard the music and needed to reassure herself that everything was all right. When she stepped in, catching her breath, Adrian was sitting on the bed reading a note. "What is it, *mijo*?"

"It's Tristan. He left a note."

Dear Adrian,

I can't explain it, but I have met a mariachi who plays beautiful music. I'm sorry, Adrian, but I have fallen in love with him. I regret having to leave you this way. I must listen to my heart. We have left to be together forever.

"Forever," Elena echoed.

Adrian dropped the note to the floor and slowly collapsed over the pillow, his eyes burning with tears. "Grandma..." Adrian's voice cracked with pain.

The old woman came and sat next to him, gently holding his hand. "I can only say that, for as long as I have lived, what will be—even beyond the grave—will be."

Adrian placed his head on the old woman's shoulder and took the long overdue chance to weep.

An emptiness overpowered Adrian's heart. His boyfriend was gone, lured by the mariachi whose *bolero* served as his bait. Who knew what would become of Tristan? At the same time, the emptiness was being replaced by guilt—for entertaining the same deceitful affair, only to have escaped it.

QUEEN OF HEARTS

What were the odds that a red queen with copious hearts would clean him out? His secret hope for a six of anything had been too optimistic, just as he suspected. Either way, his mind weighed the question one more time: What were the odds that a queen with large, vigilant eyes and oval face would clean him out?

Better yet, what were the odds that it would happen *again*, just as Cestior had done when he revealed his true heart? That's what Cestior had been: a true queen, with lucid eyes, oval face, and golden hair. Only one as brutal as Cestior could have dealt the same hand so abruptly and callously.

Again, he had lost it all.

Again, the stakes of his wager had been too high.

Eric looked distantly ahead without trying to make eye contact. The stocky man in the fedora had sat there, partly obscured by the dealer and the passing crowds. Again, he insisted on staring at Eric with his gruesome smile of sarcasm from many blackjack tables away. Without doubt, he had witnessed Eric's final bad draw.

Eric stood up, downing the remainder of his gin and tonic, his tongue savoring every bit of the bitter fizz, since his opportunity for complimentary drinks was also being terminated.

Without looking back, Eric tossed his last chip to the dealer, tipping him extravagantly. He walked past the rows of glinting, vibrant slot machines, some spewing their echoes of plausible prospects, others sitting in silence.

The instant he stepped out of the Tropicana's glass doors onto The Strip, the combination of desert-dry heated air, flickering neon, and colorful strobe lights made his head throb, aided by the bustle of crowds and zooming vehicles. The Las Vegas Strip at night was just as he had envisioned it ever since he first thought of hibernating there after his divorce from Melanie and the futile custody battle for their eight-year-old daughter Amber.

When he reached the motel he'd called home for the past two months, the scent of its shabby furniture and still air assaulted his nostrils. He examined the compressed wood walls with their golden sconces, which, once upon a time, would have successfully convinced tenants they were part of the Sin City allure. Now, they said quite the opposite, even late at night, when he peeled himself from the sheets to cool his face with splashes of water.

He wasn't sure if Cestior would be at the nightclub, exposing his smooth flesh to men for dollars atop a tiny stage barely above a hand's reach. What did Eric care, anyway? As he had told Cestior, it had ended. Did it matter that Eric hadn't even been looking for companionship, or that it had been Cestior who initially lured and pursued him? According to Cestior, he had been enamored by Eric's reserved silence and unamused eyes.

Cestior observed Eric without fail every night.

Eric would sit leaning forward at the edge of the bar, his face often immobile as he observed his surroundings. At times, only the slender billow of smoke from the cigarette wedged between Eric's fingers told Cestior Eric was alive, upright at the bar, drinking endlessly.

Eric's silence and cocky manner somehow conquered Cestior, who informed the bartender he would take care of Eric's tab. Also, he would be waiting for Eric in his dressing room near the back entrance.

Eric had only gone back there to thank Cestior. But how could he have resisted such toned legs and chiseled abs, not to mention large brown eyes and short golden curls? Cestior smiled handsomely, as if he'd never known rejection.

There, alone in the dressing room, with vanity mirrors, stage props, and bejeweled jocks, Eric watched the man everyone had been lusting after and vulgarly embracing gaze at him without blinking. He wasn't even sure what to say other than to thank him. Perhaps he should have given Cestior his drink tab money back, telling him anyone who danced there needed it more, but Cestior's large eyes and handsome features magnetized Eric. And when Cestior finally spoke, he said Eric could repay him by buying him a drink at a different bar where the two could be alone. To that, Eric nodded agreeably.

Late that night, after conversing for hours in a dim saloon with red vinyl seats and a few scruffy locals, the two made love in Eric's motel. Had Cestior not asked the right questions or not smiled timidly, as if *only* Eric existed, it would have just been hot sex. But that night, the two had made love. Eric had been seduced—completely.

❖

Everywhere Eric looked, crowds of men and even a few women packed the nightclub. Music resonated throughout, tossing its beats onto the dance floor, where a couple of strippers were gyrating above the crowd, collecting tips in their thongs.

To Eric's relief, Cestior was nowhere around, so he wouldn't see Eric's vengeful attempt at seducing some other guy. But first, he needed to be good and drunk.

Eric watched the strippers, wondering if they were as despicable as Cestior. Was their dancing just a front for how they truly made their living, just like Cestior? Were they all just waiting for tricks? That was how Eric had last caught Cestior with a man old enough to be Cestior's grandfather. To Eric's horror, it had been in the same dressing room where they had met. Now, Eric wanted nothing more than to explore Vegas and all its sinfulness the way he originally intended after leaving his old life.

Even before Eric approached his usual stool at the bar, Rob, the bartender, began preparing his gin and tonic. Eric guzzled it instantly. "Just keep them coming."

"That's actually the first time I've heard that line, if you can believe it," said the bartender.

"I always wanted to say that." Eric raised his chin, letting his guard down as he joked with the barkeep.

As the night progressed, so did the number of young men who flirted with Eric and vice versa. The drinks progressed, too. In fact, Eric was drunk again.

"Rob, tell you what!" Eric spat his words. "Here's a twenty. It's all I got. Don't let me have more drinks than I can afford, all right?"

"I hate to break it to you, man, but you've already gone way over that limit. You're drunk."

"Oh, shit!" Eric laughed. "Think I can dance to pay off the rest of my tab, just like Cestior?"

"Actually, you're in luck. Someone already has your tab covered, buddy."

Eric faced Rob, his eyes focusing. "I want nothing from him!"

"C'mon, man, don't be so harsh on him. He does love you, whether you believe that or not."

"Fuck him!" Eric pounded his fist on the bar, giving a wounded laugh. "Actually, someone is probably already fucking him right now."

"Well, guess what? Cestior isn't the one who covered your tab." Rob squeezed a lime into Eric's fresh gin and tonic.

"Yeah, right."

"No, it's true," Rob insisted, sliding the drink near Eric. "It was that strange man in the fedora hat at the end of the bar."

Eric squinted, and to his shock, it was the same man he had seen earlier at the Tropicana, observing his losing card streak. Somehow, it all made sense.

Eric let out a deep breath. "All right, let me go thank the poor bastard."

"Wait," said Rob. "I don't know about him. There's something creepy about the guy."

"He's old, stocky, and desperate. So what?"

"You're drunk, Eric. Just be careful is all I'm saying."

Eric smirked, raising his drink. Unsteadily, he weaved through the crowd to reach the other end of the bar. "I guess Vegas is a city of sin after all," Eric said as he approached the man.

"I think a city of luck is more appropriate," the man replied, arching his neck high enough so the brim of his hat permitted a full view. His voice was raspy, as if from smoking and aging. "Everything about it is based on luck, and your luck has granted you free drinks for the night."

"Thanks to you. Anyway, my luck, as you obviously witnessed, has come to an end."

"You play very daringly."

Eric grinned. "With everything."

The man nodded. "I already sensed that. A man who risks it all also has the capability to gain it all."

"You know what?" Eric took a swig from his glass before squinting and focusing. He then paused. The man's left eye appeared to shine more lustrously than the right. Also, its color was lighter and it didn't move when the man looked up at Eric. And when the man adjusted his hat, Eric counted only a pinky and thumb on his hand. The three middle fingers were missing.

The man stretched his thick, droopy lips in a grin. "You were saying something?"

"I'm sorry," Eric said, looking down at the bar momentarily. "I guess I've just been drinking a lot."

"Don't let my glass eye and/or my hand distract you. All you need to know is that tonight is *your* night. So feel free to keep drinking as much as you want."

Eric dropped his shoulders slightly. "Listen, I'm certain you're a very nice man. I just don't think I'm good company these days."

The man nodded. "I already sensed that as well. It isn't your company I'm interested in."

Eric's eyes remained fixed on the man's bizarre grin and glass eye. "I don't understand."

"I'm here because of your gambling etiquette. Indeed, you are a man who gambles aggressively. And tonight is a lucky night—for both of us."

"Wait a minute. Did my ex-wife, that bitch, send you? Or was it that queen Cestior?"

"You have quite a reputation from what I can see." The man squinted through his good eye. "Actually, nobody sent me. Tonight is only about you and your luck. I guess you could say your luck is the only thing that hasn't abandoned you, since it brought us together. I must say, you're perfect—a man so intent on winning, always so proud and unable to accept defeat. You're precisely the person I would gamble with. Indeed, you don't know how to lose."

Eric hissed his disapproval.

"And you reek of this will to win, even more than you reek of the alcohol eating at your liver."

Eric's smile froze. "I think you need to get to the fuckin' point."

"I'm going to give you three chances to win up to three million dollars. For each gamble, the stake is one million. You can leave with one, two, or all three million. That is solely up to your luck. And so far, it seems to be on the right track, considering we crossed paths."

"Okay, you're obviously crazy."

"That I am. But that doesn't mean I'm not serious."

Eric let out a deep breath before guzzling the remainder of his gin and tonic. "How can you assume I can gamble when I don't have that kind of fuckin' money?"

"Because you're not gambling with money. Only I am."

Eric's body stiffened. "Then what am I gambling with?"

"Your pride."

"Bullshit! This is bullshit! You either tell me specifically what I'm betting, or I'm outta here."

"You see, you're already losing, thanks to your pride. Your pride deprives you of this opportunity. Your pride needs to know. Well, too bad. You'll have to come with me to find out."

Eric slammed the empty glass on a small table adjacent to the man. "I'm gone. Thanks for the drinks."

Without looking back, Eric stalked past the bar, ignoring Rob, who asked if he was all right. He reached the dance floor and combated the crowd as he headed toward the exit. Looking up to get his bearings, he saw Cestior, dancing in a white lycra thong over the stage. Countless hands stretched under him, some with fluttering green bills.

Eric stopped and smiled. The two of them eyed one another, Cestior's rhythm taking on a different, slower pace. Eric rushed toward Cestior and shoved the twenty-dollar bill into Cestior's underwear as he fiercely groped Cestior's crotch. "You might as well take my last twenty! You whore!"

Cestior balanced steadily over the stage as he quickly adjusted the spandex band of his white bikini and pulled out the twenty. He looked at it sullenly before flinging it into the crowd.

Outside, a subtle stream of warm night air softly embraced Eric. It caressed him, as if the intense desert heat smothering the city all day had been nothing more than foreplay. However, it wasn't the air that was having its way with Eric. It was the liquor.

Ahead of him, the distant glowing desert city seemed small. Its casinos peeked over the desert with haloes of colors, whispering its secrets into the endless dark stretch above. Eric knew it would be a lengthy walk, but the warm air and the alcohol would keep him company all the way to his motel.

He kept thinking about the man's inane offer. It was ridiculous, but, on the other hand, what did he have to lose? According to the man, his pride. But suddenly, Eric wanted nothing more than to gamble it all, even his pride. And just as he turned, intent on returning to the nightclub, he saw the plump silhouette standing on the corner under a streetlamp, hat casting a menacing shadow. His thick smirk seemed to confirm Eric's sudden change of mind, his glass eye gleaming under the flickering streetlight.

❖

"Are you sure that's the gamble?" Eric asked. They had gone back to his motel and were now sitting on the sofa, Eric smoking the worn cigarette wedged between his long fingers.

"That is all," the man responded.

"Let me get this straight. We play three hands of blackjack. For each hand I win, you give me a million dollars. For each hand I lose, I give you the name of someone I know so you can supposedly steal their energy?"

"Not supposedly."

"That's absurd."

The man remained quiet. His serious face had become eerily visible from the small corner lamp.

"This is a waste of time. You don't even have a million dollars."

"Not on me. But whatever you win will be delivered to you first thing in the morning."

Eric let out a deep breath and nodded. "You know what? All right, you want a name? Melanie. I give you Melanie, my ex-wife. That bitch."

The man looked at Eric with his good eye. He smiled, partially concealing decaying teeth. He put his disfigured hand into his trench coat and withdrew a deck of cards, which he placed on the coffee table between them.

Eric gazed at the stack, his heart skipping a beat. And before Eric could say anything, the man shuffled the cards. He watched the man deal each of them two cards, one up and one down. Eric's was a king of spades, while the man drew a four of diamonds.

Eric turned over his second card and smiled at the queen of clubs accompanying his king. "I'll stay."

The man smiled and flipped his second card over, revealing a nine of spades. Next, he reached for another card and placed it down. A ten of spades.

Again, Eric smiled. "I guess that pushes you over twenty-one, and wins me one million dollars."

Without a word, the man recovered the cards and placed them at the bottom of the deck.

"Hey, I guess this means you won't get to absorb Melanie's energy." Eric snickered before inhaling from his cigarette. "Don't worry, it's a good thing. My ex-wife has some really bad energy on her."

"So, do you want to give me a second name?" asked the man, appearing unamused by Eric's comment.

"Me." Eric smiled. "Let's try me."

The man nodded, pressing his lips together with seriousness. Again, he dealt the cards with his disabled hand. Eric wondered how only a thumb and pinky had somehow survived. What had been the cause of his gruesome deformity? Before he knew it, Eric had received a seven of clubs and the man a nine.

When Eric turned over his other card, it was a five of diamonds. "This gives me twelve. Hit me again," he said.

To his astonishment, the queen appeared again, her heart red.

The man smiled almost obscenely, his head leaning back slightly. "I guess your energy is mine now."

Eric nodded, lips stretched in amusement. "All right, tell you what. I'll give you another name. Cestior."

The man stacked the dealt cards and placed them under the deck. Slowly, he drew the last game.

This time, Eric looked down at his queen of spades, then over at the man's four of clovers. Unsteadily, he picked up his second card, discovering a king of hearts. "Yeah! A twenty! I guess you owe me another million, mister!"

Without responding, the man turned over his second card, a six of spades. His third card was a king of diamonds. "Actually, it's a tie," he said.

"Wait a minute," said Eric. "I want a chance at winning the last game. We can't have a tie. That doesn't count."

"Suit yourself." The stranger picked up the cards and dealt them again.

Eric watched the man deal an ace of spades to himself as he gave Eric a ten of diamonds. "All right," Eric said, turning over his second card. "Eight of diamonds gives me eighteen. And I'll stay right where I am."

The man didn't answer. He adjusted his cards.

Eric smiled as he watched and waited to see what would accompany the man's ace of clubs. And when he turned over his card, it was the jack of hearts.

The man smiled. "Twenty-one."

Eric leaned back, resting against the worn sofa. He squinted as he examined the man. Casually, he inhaled the last drag of his cigarette before leaning forward and smashing the butt into the ashtray. "So, I guess my energy is going to be drained," he said, partially smiling.

The man remained silent.

Suddenly, Eric stretched his arms over his stomach and bobbed his head forward between his parted legs.

"Ahh!" he cried. "Something is wrong! I feel the energy being drained out of me. It hurts! I'm in pain!" He began to laugh uncontrollably as he looked up to face the man. "Got you, didn't I?"

To his astonishment, the room was empty. He stood up, looking around. "What the fuck!"

He scanned the room desperately, his knees weak. "Where did you go? Where the fuck are you?"

There was no response except for the silence of his empty motel room. Eric looked down at the deck on the coffee table. "What? You think I'm gonna let you take my energy? You're crazy, you hear me! You're fuckin' crazy if you think I believe any of this shit! You can go to hell!"

❖

The next morning, to Eric's disbelief, he was surrounded by heaps of hundred dollar bills stacked so high, they were falling off the worn sofa, where he had drunkenly collapsed and dreamed of Cestior.

Eric looked at all the money, sniffing the greenbacks, as if to ensure their authenticity. And when certain it was not just a dream, and the money wasn't counterfeit, he tossed a pile in the air, laughing.

It was going to be a busy day.

❖

All day, despite an upgrade to a suite overlooking The Strip, a few designer suits, and some bling, he couldn't help but think of Cestior. Eric wanted to share the news of his winnings with Cestior, but he also, in spite of everything, wanted to feel Cestior's flesh next to his.

As Eric arrived at the nightclub that night, Rob, who was talking to the bouncer near the entrance, approached him.

"Hey, Eric." The bouncer patted Eric's shoulder. "I'm sorry to have to be the one to tell you this, buddy, but Cestior had a terrible accident."

Eric swallowed, preparing himself for the next inevitable words.

"He's gone, buddy. Fell off the stage while dancing last night. No one knows how it happened. We didn't even think the fall was that bad, but it was. Apparently, he broke his neck."

Eric nodded in disbelief. Without a word, he stepped back, removing himself to the alley, where the lights were vague and the city could not reveal his fear and pain. Without a doubt, the man had murdered Cestior and would soon be looking for Eric to complete his business.

Eric rushed through the darkened and desolate streets until the silhouette he knew too well loomed several feet ahead. This time, the glass eye was no longer glass. Indeed, both eyes were different. He knew them.

They were Cestior's.

And when the man lifted his fedora and grinned at Eric, his deformed hand was in the process of regenerating its middle three fingers.

As the man's fingers grew, Eric's shrank—until they finally disappeared into his knuckles.

LOVING DEATH

Every late evening, after the sun sank beneath the high-rises facing west on Market Street, a heated aura would linger above a jagged hazy purple and orange sunset. People would move in frenzied patterns, rushing into the cabs or tunnels of the BART that zoomed inconspicuously under the city and onward. It was during this time Leonard would prepare himself, standing still with watchful brown eyes until he spotted Evan amidst the homeward-bound crowds.

This time, Evan walked slower than usual, his tall, slender frame slumped with weariness. To Leonard's surprise, Evan made a swift right on Fourth Street, veering away from Union Square before hailing a cab.

Evan's abrupt change in route stiffened Leonard with confusion. Something had changed, preventing him from his usual covert observation of Evan inside the metro transit, where Leonard would finally extend his greeting. What had changed Evan's route home from work that day?

Unsure of what to do, Leonard stood still, his eyes following the relentless Yellow Cab surging between other vehicles, until it disappeared in the traffic.

That was the last time Leonard saw Evan in San Francisco.

❖

Evan never regretted his lack of desire for memorabilia. He had brought nothing with him two years ago other than what he had been wearing. Now, his new belongings were his and only his. Everything from the dated Kenmore stove to the array of club chairs that served as the sofa surrounding his unpolished mahogany coffee table smelled of home. The potted ficus and evergreen shrub with wispy leaves served as bookends for the heaps of biographies he collected. Incense smoke billowed in the confines of his small studio's tranquility. And that tranquility was all that mattered.

He anesthetized his long day as a financial analyst for a global firm with the Chianti he sipped to ease Friday's workload stress. This glass of red would not be his last that weekend.

Later that night, he went out into the busy late evening streets of Manhattan—an island that smelled different than the ocean city he had left behind.

Manhattan was always full of Big City Life, where something as simple as another dinner alone always presented an opportunity to seclude oneself and become one with the atmosphere. This time, Evan's steak and wine combo pleased him so much, he chose to extend his night by following supper with a latte and a browse through a large bookstore on Fifth Avenue, where he would most likely purchase some sort of biography. Already he had considered buying either the biography on an acclaimed investor from the Gilded Age or an anthology of gay romances.

As he sauntered past the wall of hardbound books toward another row of mostly paperbacks, he sensed a peculiarity. Actually, he felt it first, even before he fully looked up. The man's face didn't strike him as handsome right away, but when Evan focused on his parted lips and distinctly shaped nose below large brown eyes, he felt his heart beat faster.

Leonard hadn't even expected to see him again, at least not in a bookstore. What were the odds? As if bumping into him wasn't weird enough, the stranger was soon watching Leonard with interest. Was he attracted to Leonard? That's when he knew that the guy's disappearance wasn't a coincidence. Perhaps he was meant to talk to him after all. And this time, if Leonard played his cards right, that could lead to more.

Evan had gone with the simple read and chosen the gay romances. It was the easiest book to pick up on his way to the counter, where he fumbled with his wallet before giving the cashier his debit card to swipe.

Unsure if the handsome stranger still watched, Evan casually looked behind him, but soon realized he didn't have it in him to stir up anything with anyone he found remotely attractive.

After accepting his card and the bag from the cashier, Evan left the store and walked down the paved street, where the night seemed less lively and young than before. The more he thought of the stranger, the more he felt a need to return to his studio and the walls that could insulate him from the men who always seemed to arouse his attention.

He took one step down into the street, when he slipped on some oil on the asphalt and started to fall forward. Someone grabbed him from behind and pulled him back to safety along the curb, seconds before a bus zoomed by.

Evan looked up to see the stranger from the bookstore, the very one he had shied away from.

"Are you okay?" asked Leonard.

"I...uh...I think so," Evan said. "Wow! You just saved my life!"

The stranger remained silent. Instead, he studied Evan curiously.

"You were in the bookstore," said Evan.

"So were you."

"Yeah." Evan could feel the blood rush to his face as he let out a deep breath. "God, I feel so silly. I really should watch where I'm going."

Again, the stranger didn't comment.

"Well, thanks a lot, man. I wish I knew how to repay you."

"Repay me?"

"Yeah, I even feel like offering you money or something."

Leonard smiled with a cordial chuckle. "No. No need to."

"Okay, well, thanks again," said Evan, taking a step back. "Wait a minute. I'm so rude. My name is Evan, by the way."

Leonard smiled, reaching for Evan's hand. "Leonard."

"Nice to meet you," said Evan.

"So, Evan, now that we've officially met, you really want to repay me?"

"Sure. How?"

"Join me for a stroll in Central Park."

"A walk in the park, this late?" Evan smiled. "That sounds creepy. I have a better idea. How about we go for coffee? Actually, never mind that. I've already had one, but I'm a huge caffeine fan. I drink several lattes at work, and they seem to have no impact on me."

Leonard smiled and nodded. "You lead the way."

❖

It didn't matter that Evan had already been there only hours ago, admiring the colorful burgundy and purple walls with gold molding, entrapped by the scent of coffee beans, listening to the faint jazz of Miles Davis. Everything about the quaint atmosphere seemed appropriate for Evan to play host in, especially with an attractive man who had just saved his life.

The two sat opposite one another at a small table with a view of the small terrace.

"Was there any book in particular you were interested in at the bookstore?" asked Evan.

"Not really. I guess I was just browsing."

"Yeah, I know what you mean. I had no real reason for being there other than to kill time after a lonely meal at a restaurant."

"Sorry. So, why did you move to New York?" asked Leonard.

"Huh?" Evan's eyebrows rose in suspicion. "How did you know I just moved here? Am I that obvious?"

"Not really. It's just that no one seems to be initially from New York."

"Ah," Evan said with a smile. "Well, if you must know, I moved here from San Francisco—quite abruptly, actually."

Leonard leaned back against his chair and returned Evan's smile warmly. "Abruptness is sometimes a life saver. It must have been something important."

"It was," said Evan, focusing suddenly on the wooden floor. "I was supposed to return home because he wasn't going to be there. We both planned it so I could pick up my stuff. But on my way there, I realized I didn't care about retrieving my belongings. Everything I owned had somehow become tainted by my ex-boyfriend's infidelity. In that instant, I didn't want any of it. I wanted nothing that would remind me of him, so I changed my mind at the last minute."

"Is that all that changed your mind?"

The more Evan observed Leonard's features, the more attractive they became, as if true beauty could only be detected with caution and time, like a splendid art piece whose intricate details and colors only became truly alive with study. Every time Evan gazed in Leonard's eyes, his throat tightened. He had to look away before answering Leonard's question.

"I don't even know. It was sort of weird, actually. I just had this strange feeling, like a premonition, that if I went home I would never leave San Francisco, or even worse, I would regret something deeply. And for the first time in my life, I followed my instincts and made a sharp turn to the airport, bringing only the clothes I wore."

"Did your ex-boyfriend try reaching you after that? I'm sure he wondered if you would ever pick up your stuff."

"He called my parents' home and mailed everything to them, but I still don't care to have them back."

"Good choice," said Leonard, sliding his hand closer to Evan's closed fist. "Indeed, at times abrupt changes are the best ones."

Evan smiled and nodded, allowing Leonard's warm hand to wrap around his.

❖

Perhaps it had been Leonard's tender touch or his speed in saving Evan's life, but for the first time since leaving San Francisco, Evan allowed himself to trust.

The two began to meet for strolls in Central Park or for coffee and dessert at various spots in Greenwich Village. During one of their meetings, Leonard proved New York was not so lonely after all.

He had smiled and, without warning, kissed Evan. The kiss lasted long enough for the old wounded Evan to consider it a rude display of affection. But enamored Evan indulged in Leonard's soft, thick lips. All that mattered to Evan was savoring the intensity of their warmth. They tasted of earth and sky, other elements conjoined and harvested, like clear waters and organic evergreens meshed with stars.

❖

Every evening the two men met was arranged without telephone numbers or addresses. Evan decided to overlook that peculiarity due to the mystique it added. The next date would come from the first.

"How about a sundae on a Sunday?" Leonard asked unexpectedly one day.

"Huh? Sunday on a Sunday?"

"Ice cream. How about ice cream on Sunday afternoon?"

"Sure," Evan said with a smile. "Where?"

"There." Leonard pointed to a place with a quaint pink-and-white canopy.

❖

During their date on Sunday at the charming pastry and gelato café, Evan realized how much of their conversation always revolved around him. Whenever Leonard spoke of himself, it was only about current activities and objects, such as the canopy or the white metal French chairs with heart-shaped cords supporting their backs.

"I've always liked these Parisian-looking chairs," said Leonard.

"Where did you say you were from?" asked Evan, slightly sliding his strawberry sundae toward Leonard.

"Vanilla and cotton candy." Leonard nodded and smiled.

"Huh?"

"Vanilla and cotton candy," Leonard repeated, looking up at the wallpaper. "That's what these little French cafés remind me of. I wasn't sure why, but now I know. It's the white and pink. It reminds me of French vanilla ice cream and pink cotton candy. That's why these cafés always utilize this setup. It's to entice customers to buy expensive desserts, even before they've thought about it."

"Leonard…" said Evan, his hands together as he leaned against the rounded table's edge. "You're ignoring my question."

"I'm just saying it reminds me of dessert."

"Okay, so answer my question. Where are you from?"

"I'm *not* from New York."

"Okay, from where?"

"Evan, to be honest, I don't care much to talk about myself. I'm just really interested in learning all there is to learn about *you*. I think you're a fascinating guy."

"But I don't know much about you," Evan said. "Where you live, where you're from, or even what it is that you do.

Do you ever work? I mean, you seem to have an awful lot of free time."

Leonard let out a deep breath, facing the wallpaper. "As a matter of fact, I *do* work. Excuse me for making time for you. Also, excuse me for wanting to know more about you."

"Listen," Evan said, "I don't mean to come off intrusive and suspicious. It's just that I want to know more about *you*. I don't think it's fair I've shared so much of myself and know nothing about you. I don't have your phone number. Heck, I don't even know where you live."

"Neither do I." Leonard smiled. "Why does everything have to be demystified so quickly between two people? It sort of takes the fun out."

Evan leaned back, pressing his lips tightly, as if to refrain from saying something he would regret. But then he spoke. "Leonard, when it comes to taking things slowly, believe me, I'm in that boat. I don't want something serious. Hell, I don't care much that we haven't had sex. I don't want a boyfriend or a lover, at least not now. But if we are hanging out, personal questions are a given. Besides, wanting to know a little more about you isn't really pushing any romantic envelope. Actually, in this day and age, it's called *precaution*. It's important to know one's surroundings so one does not cross paths with a lunatic."

"Are you calling me a lunatic?"

"No! Leonard, jeez…All I'm saying is that one cannot be so naïve and trusting, and I just want to know more about you. That's all."

Leonard remained silent. He gazed blankly at Evan, before looking out the arched window that showcased a lazy Sunday afternoon on Madison Avenue.

"You know what? I'm not much in the mood for a sundae on a Sunday anymore," said Evan, pushing back his chair and standing up. "I think it's best if I go."

"Evan…I don't lie. I always tell the truth, which is why I am hesitant to let you know more about me. You wouldn't understand."

"Try me," said Evan, his tone cold and serious.

"Evan, it isn't that simple."

"Would you prefer I just leave? It's not like you have my number or know where I live, or vice versa. If I leave here, what are the odds we'll bump into each other again?"

Leonard looked down. "All right, Evan. But let's not do it here. Let us take a walk."

Once again, the two men headed into Central Park, where the warm afternoon sun blended its rays with the still air and the unmovable greens.

"Okay," said Evan, "what is it you feel I wouldn't understand about you, Leonard?"

"I do have a job. But it doesn't pay the bills or sustain my means to live. My job is different."

Evan could feel his frustration increase with every passing second. "What are you? A drug dealer or something? Big deal."

"No."

"Then what? Just say it already."

"I'm a guide for the dead."

"The dead? You mean you're a mortician. You work at a morgue, right?"

"No. I guide the Departed. I present myself when men are dying, and I wait until they are fully dead so I can guide them to where they need to go."

It didn't matter that the sun shone or the birds chirped in the distance. Evan's knees became weak, and his blood turned cold.

"That's right, Evan. Destiny brought me to guide you even before you left San Francisco. You were supposed to get on the metro to collect your belongings, not in that cab."

"Wait a minute. How did you know about the subway and the cab?"

"That evening, you weren't going to make it home. Written destiny predicted a thief aboard the subway was supposed to take your life. What is written is always what the eventual outcome will be, but somehow you avoided your fate. It also happened the day of the bookstore. You were supposed to be hit by that bus, but I intervened. I shouldn't have. I am not meant to be seen or to interfere. But I made myself visible so I could be with you. I don't know what my price is for interfering with written destiny, but I had to. I found you fascinating. I wanted to know more about you before I guided you away from Earth. I wanted to know what it was like to be seen by you, the same way you see other men, and even the way you kiss them. I am intrigued by you. Actually, I'm in love with you, Evan. And I do not lie."

Stunned, Evan didn't answer. He stood dumbfounded, his lips glued together, without the strength to form words.

"Please don't be scared, Evan." Leonard raised his hand in an attempt to caress Evan's cheek, but stopped the instant Evan jerked back. "I'm sorry, Evan. I really am."

"Get away from me," Evan said as he continued stepping back. "You're a freak! You hear me! You're a fuckin' freak!"

"Evan, wait!" Leonard watched Evan run into the park until he could no longer trace him. He remained still, watching only the distant high-rises, all aligned and constantly humming with lives within. Somewhere in that humming, one of the voices stung his ears. It was time again to perform his job for a stranger. At least he wouldn't have to think about Evan.

❖

Attempting to forget Leonard over the next twenty-five years hadn't been easy for Evan.

He remembered Leonard mostly in his last few years, when he was at a hospital lamenting a dying friend or family member. He'd wonder if Leonard was wandering the ICU halls, waiting. Thoughts of Leonard would also surface when an ambulance would rush by, or even during the few times any fatality occurred around Evan.

This time, it was *his* fatality.

Who would have thought the small engine plane would plummet into the foreign desert regions of Dubai? Intense pain all over came the second he heard the noises of the crash. Next came the taste of blood in his throat and lungs. Evan felt the blood that would kill him first. As for his body, he wouldn't dare to look, in fear of discovering he'd been dismembered. It wasn't the way he wanted to see himself for the very last time.

He knew it was too late the moment it started to get dark despite the harsh sun that penetrated beyond the distant hills. It was over when he saw Leonard, looking the same as Evan remembered him: large brown eyes and bulbous lips, the ones that had tasted of earth's purest elements. Leonard appeared angelic and unmarked by age.

Leonard smiled at Evan, caressing his face slowly, as if blood and pain were nonexistent, just as Evan would soon no longer exist.

"I'm sorry, Evan."

"Take me away, Leonard," Evan whispered. "Take me with you, please."

THE MASTABA OF NIANKHKHNUM

Every individual grain of desert sand was changing color, becoming less pallid and even more compressed near the Saqqara. After countless ridges stretching endlessly for miles, it was a sign the necropolis was finally near. The distant step pyramid of Djoser and the nearby Uran were already visible ahead, standing with the same royalty they had possessed thousands of years ago.

The endless sky was pale and heated with the scent of the unburied, alive, and imperishable Old Kingdom and its histories, just like the tomb they were scouting.

Nestor could feel the sand in his most intimate places, like between his toes or in his scalp. He should have been happy in the back seat of the Jeep, riding with the caravan of archeologists, headed up by his boyfriend Trevor, whose translation of the Old Kingdom history and its artifacts had led them to the eldest civilization of Egypt.

But somehow, the sand always managed to sneak its way into Nestor's clothing, irritating him, plaguing him until the very end of another lengthy research or excavation work day. He couldn't wait for Trevor's smile to announce it was the end of the day. Trevor would also be dirty, sand creeping into his golden hair, smudging his neck and the rims of his glasses.

If Nestor had remained in the hotel, enjoying the local sights and museums as Trevor had suggested, none of the desert's discomforts would have bothered him. But Nestor wanted to be the supportive boyfriend, since it was Trevor who'd brought him to Egypt. If the necropolis of the Saqqara was important to Trevor, then it may as well be important to Nestor, even if all he did was watch and occasionally aid the team by taking notes as they studied the translation of chambers and elaborate hieroglyphics.

"So, should we begin to look for an area where we could set up a station?" Monica, another archeologist, asked Trevor, who was driving.

"Actually, let's continue heading a little more south, closer to the escarpment," Trevor said. "It'll be easier near the slope of the plateau."

"Ah, that makes sense!" said Andrew, the oldest member of the team. "I understand the tomb was discovered in the mid 1960s."

"1964, to be exact," Trevor said with a smile. "This Fifth Dynasty tomb of Niankhkhnum and Khnumhotep was discovered under the direction of Mounir Basta and Ahmed Mousa. It's one of the largest and most beautiful tombs in Saqqara's entire necropolis. And it was built for these two men with identical titles in the palace of King Niusere of the Fifth Dynasty. The men wanted to be joined in life as well as in death."

"And they got their wish," Monica quipped.

"'*Hotep*,' meaning peace," Trevor said, winking at Nestor in the rearview mirror. "The desire of these two men to remain together in this life as well as the next was true and imperishable. It's tenderly romantic if you ask me."

Nestor pursed his lips, raising his eyebrows in sarcasm. "Cute, but truly homoerotic if you ask me. What were these men's *titles*, anyway?"

"They were manicurists," Monica answered.

"Manicurists!" Nestor laughed. "Even in ancient Egypt we didn't spare our gayness!"

"Not in the way you imagine, Nestor," said Andrew. "They groomed King Niusere. They were the king's administrators and confidants, Prophets of Ra. Besides, can't you see your honey is only trying to impress you? If my wife were here, I would have said the same thing."

"Not the same," Nestor said. "At least not with the words 'manicurist' or 'grooming King Niusere' in your sentence."

"Well, despite your boyfriend's aim at romanticizing this Mastaba," Monica said, "professors have been attempting to debunk the assumption these men were homosexual. It's been said they were identical twins, and that's why the pictorial records appear so intimate."

The Jeep motored slowly down the slope, eventually halting at the base of the tomb. Nestor noticed how removed it was from the other monuments, surrounded by ridges of sand from previous excavations. It perched with complete superiority, slanting slightly on all four sides, as if it could have formed a pointy pyramid if it was higher. It appeared to have a masculine nature.

Nestor admired it with awe, including the vaguely visible slabs of stone forming a path around the tomb before falling victim to sandstorms and natural forces.

Its entrance was flanked by two cut-stone pillars with hieroglyphics on their slanted edges.

"These are their names, symmetrically inscribed on the architraves," said Trevor. "Let's step into the vestibule."

Nestor followed slowly behind the team, which had powered up the high-end lighting equipment. He took a deep breath, but his chest felt heavy. He wasn't sure, but something about the tomb made him feel weary and nervous. Although he was becoming used to the scent of such stone rooms and ceilings, the air in this crypt felt more condensed.

"It's quite muggy in here," said Monica.

"It sure is," Nestor agreed. "Whoever said the scent of death dissolves after thousands of years was certainly wrong. I'm sure their tombs still reek."

"Actually, there are no elaborate sarcophagi or glamorous objects in here," said Trevor. "We're here solely to explore the carved histories on the walls and courtyard. And if I'm not mistaken, they should be somewhere past this corridor."

Nestor moved in slowly, gripped by the illustration of the two men carved into the rock near the entrance. They sat closely with their arms wrapped around each other's shoulders. To his surprise, another illustration on the southern side of the wall boldly displayed the two men walking while holding hands.

"Ah, there they are!" said Trevor, his voice echoing within the tomb. "This one near the entrance is their way of welcoming visitors, a friendly gesture for visiting *The House of Eternity*. The other one, at least what remains of it, is Niankhkhnum leading Khnumhotep into the tomb. Perhaps Niankhkhnum was the more dominant one."

"This is phenomenal!" Monica enthused, shoving a strand of blond hair behind one ear. "Truly breathtaking."

Nestor couldn't remove his eyes from the affectionate display of the two men. How could a pharaoh who once reigned over Egypt have allowed two men to expose such intimacies in public? His heart skipped a beat, and he felt lightheaded, overwhelmed with pleasure at something so hidden in the corners of the earth.

"Now this is what I call buried history," said Andrew.

"Let's move forward," said Trevor, leading the team. "Ahead is a smaller room, but you won't see any colorful illustrations. Now, to our right, past this small corridor, is the courtyard."

Nestor followed the team into an enclosed area fully lit with sunlight that filtered through a screened ceiling. The two men appeared again, each one illustrated colorfully on opposite sides of the perfectly square-cut entryway to the courtyard.

Stepping down the blocky stone, they all stood in the center of the courtyard, admiring the fine cut-stone with its sporadic glyphs.

"It's so serene in here," said Monica. "Like a private atrium."

"Indeed, it is," Trevor agreed. "We're surrounded by stone except for the lattice ceiling. That door on the south end should lead us into a second small vestibule, followed by the rock-cut chapel."

Nestor looked up, the sunlight blinding him into darkness for an instant. When he opened his eyes again, the images appeared three-dimensional, like a montage—including a tall man standing watch near the entryway, stiff like a palace guard or statue.

Nestor jerked back, bumping his shoulder against Trevor's side.

"Wow, are you okay?"

Nestor didn't answer. His eyes remained wary as he examined the courtyard.

"It must be the heat," said Monica.

"No, I'm fine," said Nestor.

"All right, then," Trevor continued. "Now, if I'm not mistaken, there's a small room called the chapel and another called the offering room, and they are that way," he said, pointing.

Nestor waited for everyone to step into the vestibule. Above its entryway was a stone, shaped like a cylinder with hieroglyphics. Nestor knew well enough that it emulated a rolled-up mat, which in ancient times was used to seal doors and provide privacy.

They stepped into a long, rectangular room full of illustrations on the stone walls. The two men were pictured in various activities, such as feasting on offerings and being entertained by dancers, clappers, and musicians. Something about the artwork made his heart throb and ache, as if he was missing something or someone.

"The craftsmanship here is magnificent," said Monica.

"It's more than that," said Trevor. "As you can see, all these walls are embellished with pictures of everything from agriculture to carpentry and even domestic life. On the southern end of this chapel are two entryways, both leading into the offering room."

Nestor understood why these intimate portrayals in the offering room created such debate amongst professors and historians. Again, the two men stood closely, facing each other, this time their noses touching, their arms and hands fastened together. Their torsos were so close, the string belts from their loincloths appeared to touch, perhaps were even knotted together.

"As you can see, this image is a relief: the two men between two façade doors." Trevor's voice penetrated the enclosure, and he pointed to the opposite wall. "Another image, quite the same as the one we were just looking at, signifies the same thing. It signifies the men's—"

"'—Eternal Embrace,'" Nestor said, hypnotized by the figures.

"Exactly," said Trevor. "Wait. How did you know that?"

"You already told us," said Andrew.

"No, I haven't."

"I just know it," said Nestor. "My heart told me so."

"Okay," said Monica, facing all three men. "We have plenty of work to do here. So let's get to it, gentlemen."

Even after the team stepped out, Nestor remained inside the chapel, exploring the meticulous carvings and color of the two men. Nestor stood still, enjoying his privacy, as if he had discovered serenity within the deepest compartment of the world.

He slowly caressed the mighty ancient chiseled figures. The mounds of his fingertips slid against their hands and arms, but he felt a faint sheet of moisture between the stone and his skin as he traced the naked chest of Niankhkhnum. It was hot inside the tomb, but this did not seem natural. Nestor drew his fingers away from the inexplicable feel of moisture over the artwork. Putting his face against the face of the rock, he sniffed at it.

The moisture smelled of flowers.

He looked up, focusing on Niankhkhnum's eyes, which steadfastly remained on his partner, Khnumhotep. For an instant, they seemed to be looking down, directly at Nestor, thoroughly examining him. Nestor's heart jolted as he felt something coil around his neck, but it was only Trevor's arm.

"Are you okay?"

"I'm fine," Nestor said, his tone defensive.

"Are you sure?"

"I said I was fine."

"Hey, lovebirds," said Andrew, stepping into the offering room, "Monica needs Nestor to help edit her notes."

"Let's do it," Nestor answered. He looked back only briefly at the carving, which appeared no longer moist but dry as the rest of the walls.

❖

It wasn't until late at night that the four of them regrouped in the lobby of their Cairo hotel.

"So did everyone take a long bath and a nice nap?" asked Andrew, clasping a glass of brandy as he stretched his back lazily against a rococo carved chair of dark hewn wood.

"Have they stopped serving dinner?" Monica asked, her black cocktail dress partially exposing her alabaster shoulders. Her silk dress swayed below her knees, in cadence with the live piano music.

"No, I just checked," Trevor said, adjusting the cufflinks on his white shirt.

"I'm certainly starving," Monica added. "We'll have to find something."

❖

Even after their meal, hours past their long day of research and archiving, Nestor could still vividly recall the images in the tomb every time he shut his eyes. He expected they would even show up in his dreams, just as such images and insignias always did after intense concentration. But mostly, he couldn't stop thinking about Niankhkhnum—his chiseled flesh and nearly naked body. It even followed him out onto the balcony from the bar lounge, where he left everyone behind with the rest of the hotel crowd.

He felt the bustling city of Cairo at night below him. Darkness and lights intertwined with the sounds of vehicles and voices. Above him the myriad stars were moderately visible, shared by the city and desert. The distant desert, as impenetrable as the stars above, watched him. It was as if the two went hand in hand—desert and stars—feeding off one another. He thought of how both stretched beyond Cairo, with its serpent river and ancient secrets. And he thought of Niankhkhnum. All day long, Niankhkhnum had watched Nestor from room to room as he had taken notes, accompanied by the team.

Nestor gazed again at the city below, looking up once more at the stars, as if they connected him with Niankhkhnum. The thought of it soothed his heart. He thought of Niankhkhnum's tomb, the ancient images colorfully alive. Only then did he realize his yearning for Niankhkhnum.

With his index finger, Nestor gently traced the silhouette of the manicurist over the handrail. He had learned the shape quite well, a frame always next to his male companion. Indeed, their embrace had become eternal for everyone to watch, even thousands of years later.

Again, Nestor gazed down at the street, where locals still scurried along the sidewalks. To his surprise, he noticed he was being watched. In the crowd stood a tall, slender figure gazing up in Nestor's direction. It stood still, unperturbed by the hustle of people on bicycles and mopeds. Had it not been so dark and crowded, Nestor could have gotten a better view of the figure.

But an old woman with a basket balanced on her head nearly collided with a biker, and as they both parted, Nestor saw the figure clearly for a few seconds. It was the manicurist, complete with ancient garments and necklace.

Nestor's knees stiffened before they became weak. His blood turned from warm to cold, chilling his insides instantly. He continued gazing at the figure, which became obscured again by people and shadows. When they cleared, the figure was nowhere to be seen. It was as if the pedestrians had swallowed him. Had it been a mirage? Somehow, the ancient pictographs were sneaking into his night world.

❖

The next morning, Nestor decided not to share it with Trevor or any of the other archeologists. Instead, Nestor's heart told him that his sighting of an ancient Prophet of Ra and trustee to royalty should remain unshared and personal, as if the entire day spent studying him on frescoed or sculpted walls, like no one before, had been sacred.

Again, within the tomb of the Saqqara, Nestor took dictation from Monica, Andrew, and Trevor. And every time Nestor's eyes met Niankhkhnum's, Nestor gazed at him differently, as if aware the manicurist watched him, too.

Sometime during midday, Nestor stepped into the courtyard, where light from the sun seeped through the woven mesh ceiling. He remembered how he'd imagined seeing a figure along the edge of the rectangular stone-cut entrance when he had first set foot in this private atrium.

He observed the courtyard's confidentiality and precise workmanship. He couldn't help but picture the men who embedded the stones, and who all along knew this structure would memorialize two male companions. The manicurists were chiseled so artfully, it had to have been done by someone who thought about their affection for each other, accepted it, and honored it royally and religiously.

Nestor had become so consumed by his thoughts, he wasn't aware of the hand suddenly coiling around his neck. It startled him, causing him to jerk back before realizing it was Trevor.

"Jesus!" Nestor hissed. "You startled me!"

"Sorry, I was just trying to be affectionate. Are you okay?"

"I'm fine."

"Are you sure? You look flushed."

"Well, what do you expect? After startling me like that!"

"Poor baby," said Trevor, wrapping his hands around Nestor's waist. "A kiss will make it better."

"Wait."

"What's wrong?"

"Nothing. I just feel weird. This place is sacred, and we need not disrespect it."

"Are you kidding me with this?" Trevor snorted.

"I just…I don't know. I guess I'm just hot. Too much sun."

"You want to take a nap or something?"

"No, I'm fine." Nestor glanced briefly at Niankhkhnum alongside the entrance that led farther into the tomb. It was as if the manicurist was watching.

"Are you sure? You know the chapel is a little cooler, since it's close to the courtyard. Really, baby, you should rest. The three of us are occupied with the interpretations in the first room, and we won't disturb you." Trevor reached for Nestor's hands, squeezing them and bringing them to his lips.

Nestor glanced one more time at Niankhkhnum. "You know something? I think I do need to rest. This place is really taking a toll on me. I think I'm done for the day."

"That's great. I'll go to the Jeep and bring you a blanket to use for padding."

"Thanks," Nestor said, and kissed Trevor on the lips.

Nestor hadn't realized how tired he'd become until making himself comfortable alongside the southern end of the chapel. His body curved slightly, facing the two entryways to the offering room. It wasn't long before the images returned, living vividly in his world of darkness. He saw the almond-shaped eyes of these men and heard their whispered story of passion and past—two men joined eternally, even in the afterlife, and even then, still watching. Niankhkhnum always watching.

Nestor fell into a deep sleep.

❖

At first, Nestor wasn't sure why he felt warm. A distant golden aura began expanding as he opened his eyes. He was inside the tomb, but the chapel was surrounded by lit torches. Why would the team place lighted torches inside the tomb when they had electric gadgets to light the place?

Nestor sat up, realizing the blanket was missing. Something was definitely different. "Trevor?"

He stood up and walked into the vestibule, which was also torchlit. Night had arrived in the courtyard with a slender, chalky moon.

"Where is everyone?" Nestor asked. "Trevor?" His voice echoed nervously, bouncing off the walls before escaping into the dark sky above.

He bolted to the next room, which was also empty and lit by torches, then raced to the main entrance, where the first vestibule led the way out. To his horror, it was sealed shut. A thick concrete door had been placed over it.

"What the hell is going on?" His voice trembled, even as he called out for Trevor once again.

Desperately, he looked around the vestibule. The images of Niankhkhnum and his partner were the only ones that surrounded him. "Trevor!"

He stepped back into the first room, the images he knew so well even more colorful under torchlight, as if freshly created and showcased at their best.

At first, he thought the figure was just another shadow coming to life from the wavering torch flames. But it wasn't. The tall, stiff figure was cornered inside the small side room, where the lights from the flames barely reached. It was watching Nestor with gleaming eyes. Nestor wanted to scream, but his strength had suddenly diminished the instant his blood turned cold, rushing down to his feet.

The figure continued to watch, even as it took one step forward, its naked shoulders and broad chest coming into the light. A thick, gold, oval necklace plate reflected opulently above its squared pecs.

Nestor knew what he was seeing. Somehow, it had all become real, from the sandals that strapped below his brawny calves to the short loincloth that exposed his muscular thighs.

"Niankhkhnum," he whispered. His eyes widened, filling with utter horror as the Egyptian manicurist clutched a long, sharp blade and advanced on Nestor.

Petrified, Nestor ran into the courtyard—and stumbled. His body lay stiff, the moon watching from above. He felt pain from his knees to his elbows.

"Help!" he cried, his voice escaping into the night. "Help me, somebody!"

He got to his feet, facing the ancient figure and its acute blade. He ran into the second vestibule and back into the chapel, then continued toward the end, where the two doors led into the offering room.

Nestor halted in horror, attempting to make sense of what he saw under the torch flames lighting the small room. He recognized the short blond hair and glasses on the decapitated head in seconds. "Trevor!"

The other heads rested nearby, and now, it was *his* turn to join the team—their heads perfectly aligned on the offering room floor.

Before he could gather his thoughts, the tall figure was already behind him, raising the blade. Just as he was about to shout out the ancient being's name, another figure came into view. Niankhkhnum!

He had been wrong. The figure chasing him was Khnumhotep.

This one in front of him was Niankhkhnum, holding a long sword with a sharp and bloodied blade.

Before Nestor could even prepare himself, he watched the sword's swift descent in terror. But it had descended on Khnumhotep instead. Khnumhotep's head spiraled downward, landing over the others, its blood splattering on the stone floor.

Nestor wanted to scream, but the shock of Niankhkhnum reaching out for him froze him instantly. Niankhkhnum gripped Nestor's wrist. Slowly, he brought Nestor's hand over his chest, allowing it to gently caress his flesh.

Niankhkhnum gazed down at Nestor, just like Nestor remembered from the walls—the way they had all along gazed into Nestor's eyes. And even amidst the dread and horror, Nestor felt the ancient manicurist's chest and neck, just as he had done the day he first encountered the carving of the Mastaba.

Niankhkhnum uttered words of an ancient language, but Nestor understood them very well: "The time has come for you to join me in eternity."

THE ARCHANGEL'S CANVAS

You see, Adam was also an angel," the fortune-teller had said. "However, once upon a time, Michael lost his fire, and Adam escaped becoming a part of the mundane world. Adam was the first, and Michael swore to himself he would never rest until he found Adam and reunited with him."

"That's absurd!" I laughed in her face. "What are you gonna say next, that Lucifer desperately waits for the day Raphael becomes evil and joins him in the fiery pits of Hell?"

The tarot reader clearly found no humor in my interpretation of her prediction. "Not exactly. Michael is cursed due to a violation of pleasure in the heavens, and it is he who awaits Adam still. He won't disclose to you who he is right away. Instead, he will tell you it is your beauty that drew him to you. But he lies."

She was talking in circles.

"Whatever," I said, rising from my chair so abruptly, I nearly tipped it over. "This was a total waste of time and money!"

❖

I nodded to myself, swallowing the bitter residue of espresso left on my palate. I looked over and smiled at the inane sight of a rendezvous developing at one of the corner tables opposite of where I had planted myself.

He had been sitting alone, waiting, not much different from me, his brown eyes focusing intently on what lay ahead.

I could tell from their greeting and hug the two had never before met. Perhaps it was the result of an internet connection supplemented by a chain of emails, or a setup between friends. They were prowling shamelessly, meeting in public with hopes of beginning something that promised nothing. I was certain of it. I was free to judge, for I had tried it once myself, years ago.

Sliding my mug away, I glanced at my watch to make sure I wasn't late for the art gallery unveiling where I was photographing and critiquing the work of an Italian artist named, coincidentally, Michael. He had no last name, but he *did* have a taste for nouveau angels.

As I prepared to leave, I felt someone looking at me. I was being watched and perhaps judged, as I had been judging. I finally spotted him at a distant corner table in a dimmer part of the coffeehouse. He, too, sat alone. He rested his chin on his thumb and kept his eyes on me. He didn't smile or look away as I stared at him boldly. My plan to stare him down failed the moment I looked into his pupils—obscure and intriguing gray-browns. They intimidated me, compelling me to look down.

His eyes blazed at me before switching to the couple I had been watching. But then they returned to me, and mine to his, recklessly.

At first I imagined them as spheres in flame, but I was wrong. He had been watching and judging me, and I couldn't look away. He had read my thoughts. Suddenly, all that mattered to me was the opinion in his golden-gray eyes, ones that could only be seen on an archangel of fire. I couldn't help but envision him as Michael, the Archangel of Fire.

He smiled, exposing a perfect white strip beneath his pink lips. Despite the alluring spectacle, I refrained from flirting and blushing. Instead, I walked out into the cold night, tucking my fists into my coat, my heart aching for more of what had just occurred. I knew those eyes and that handsome face would haunt me for days.

❖

Inside the gallery, the spacious walls were filled with colorful canvases of reds, whites, purples, and other vivid colors swirled and meshed together but spaced so you couldn't analyze or absorb them too quickly. The array was meant to be observed with time and precision so their alluring mysticism erupted with a conjoined force of color blends, angles, and chiaroscuros.

I flashed my Canon between the heads of people as I eavesdropped on the curator and the occasional dignitary.

A tall, slender woman with slick black hair and a matching gown squeezed between me and a couple who stood mesmerized by a large red canvas.

With a hand over her chest, she observed my camera and spoke. "I've been fascinated with his art since his last exhibit in Venetia! All of his pieces are simply…fascinating, the way each one has been painted in a different country. His collections have toured through Prague, Paris, Amsterdam, and other countries where Western art reigns. So you can only imagine when I heard he and his art would be here, in downtown Long Beach, of all places, I simply died."

"Excuse me? Have you met him?"

"You mean Michael no-last-name?"

"That's right. I'm here reviewing his art. I didn't know he was making a personal appearance here in Long Beach."

"Why, yes, and he's as handsome as his art!" She gestured to the red piece before us. "Simply look at the way those two red angles clash with the white, reddened and alive, as if the white is succumbing to the apex above. His colors are a combination of strange symbiosis. I heard this one came to life in Morocco. I could only dream of what inspired him. Isn't he the best?"

I remained still, realizing I hadn't detected the obvious beauty of the colors, and her perceptions somewhat crushed me. After all, who was I to critique someone whom I hadn't even the slightest clue was making an appearance? Feeling shameful, I looked down at my camera and notepad and whispered to myself, "Time to be professional, Adam."

"Michael!" the slender female yelped, her index finger directing into the crowd.

Nothing could have surprised me more than when I spotted him. He was the same handsome figure with the alluring eyes I'd seen at the café.

He glanced over, as if aware we were observing him. With one hand in the pocket of his dark slacks, he ambled toward us, no visible emotion on his face. He reached for one of the glasses of red wine on its silver tray.

"My art is better admired and understood with wine," he said, eyeing me directly as he extended the wine glass. He had a faint accent I couldn't identify.

I looked to my right, expecting the slender female to notice my blushing, but to my joyous surprise, she had flitted away to annoy someone else. I was left alone with Michael.

I grabbed the wine he offered, eyeing him intently as I extended my hand. "Thank you very much. It's an honor."

"You see, being drunk is the only way one can make sense of this shit." He laughed regally, his voice deep and masculine.

I shook my head in disagreement. "It's excellent. Allow me to introduce myself. I'm Adam. You came directly from your show in Italy, I'm assuming."

He looked at my camera and notepad. "Yes. It's pleasant, this city. But please, enjoy my art, Adam. And in your review, be harsh if you must, but be honest." He disappeared into the crowd.

"Isn't he a doll?" the slender woman asked, having suddenly rushed back.

I didn't answer. Instead, I sipped the red. I could tell from its oak aftertaste the wine had been barreled especially for that precise taste.

I allowed myself to become lost in the crowd and savor the dry potency of the red. My senses felt heightened, as if I could truly savor and depict every ingredient in the wine. My head became light, and my desire for him grew. Every sip tantalized, stirring a craving for his voice and another look into his alluring eyes. I began getting occasional glimpses of those eyes in the crowd, and I was able to hear the echoes of his deep voice over the laughter of his guests.

As for his art, indeed there was something even more vivid about it with wine. The colors became alive. Reds and deep purples watched me. Their sashaying vibrancy seemed to breathe with life, as if the mixture of colors had flavor—*his* flavor, or the same taste I savored from the wine—and then, another glimpse.

Watching him from a distance, I became spellbound by the slight part of his lips. His smile had a certain cockiness that seduced me. I remained behind as the crowd began to scatter. The wine was gone, but the taste of him remained on my lips. I craved more. I think my desire was no secret to him, for he gripped my wrist with his cold hand, his warm lips behind my neck.

"Show me your city," he said.

"It's cold and late," I said, facing him, "but there's nothing I'd rather do than show you."

We stepped out into a cold night. Instantly, the chilly air awakened my senses, quickly diluting the effect of the wine. As we stood closely, I focused on his broad shoulders, the slant of his jaw, his pale cheekbones—which looked both soft and bristly. I sensed their "beardly effect" would be sensual roughness from each side. Close up, his eyes had a transparent gray around his honey-colored pupils. He wore a vibrant ruby ring on his pinky finger, which he suddenly intertwined—along with the rest of his fingers—with mine. I wasn't sure where we were headed. I didn't care.

The dark, moist streets were empty of people. We walked side by side slowly, without speaking. We didn't need words for our extraordinary bond.

He paused and faced me below a dim streetlight. He rested his hands on either side of my face and studied me closely. He suddenly, savagely locked his lips on mine. He tasted of the oak in the red, and I wanted more. He squeezed me against his solid chest. I welcomed his thrusting tongue, savoring him until he pulled back and smiled. He directed my gaze to the golden lights of the surrounding high-rises on Ocean Boulevard.

"It's a beautiful skyline at night," I said. "And if you close your eyes, you can smell the ocean nearby."

"Please," he whispered into my ear. "Let me tell you something about my creative process." His warm breath encircled my neck. "You see, I wasn't sure if I would find something in the city that would inspire me—until I saw you."

"The café."

"Yes. Your observation and your scorn of others. You fascinate me. You see, I understand you. It takes many years of being alone to think as we do. And it takes an observer of the night's darkness and other people's shadows to detect another. Even though you have been in your solitude for only a few years compared to me, you are equipped with the same mind."

I yearned to make sense of his words, yet I knew he had spoken the truth. He had been able to read my mind back at the café. I pretended to act surprised, but this stranger who meshed colors knew me. And now he welcomed me to his exclusive world.

"Join me in my accommodations," he said. "I'm staying at a small place that overlooks the dark ocean and the city."

Without words, I followed him to one of Long Beach's most historic and familiar tall buildings, Villa Riviera. I loved its exterior intricate stone carvings and gargoyles. The roof lights showcased its towering green roof, the moon adding an additional intensity. It stood still and oblique, like a night creature looking back at us from afar.

When we stepped inside, I noted the Villa Riviera's preserved, or revived, moldings that framed its high ceilings as well as the elevator that opened for us.

When we reached his suite, I gasped at the striking view of the whirling ocean. I faced the open balcony window, taking in the scent of sea and cool air as I felt the soft caress of his hands over my back. Despite my buzz from the wine and his charm,

I felt more alive than ever, looking down at the glistening, thrashing waves.

His spacious master suite was wide, with a separate living room showcasing tall Oriental porcelain vases and art deco floor lamps. We entered the large bedroom, which boasted a high, bolstered bed and silken bedspread. He had stacked leather steamer trunks alongside the mattress, but they didn't look nearly as out of place as the easel nearby.

The canvas on it was blank, as if it had been waiting for Michael to decide on the precise moment to illustrate yet another one of his worlds. Michael looked over at me and smiled. "Can you feel it?" Michael asked, leaning forward. "It yearns for my embrace because it hungers for you—your secrets and your pose. It wants to re-create you."

I swallowed deeply, eyeing the canvas as if it were human and watching us like a third being.

Michael rested his hands on my shoulders. "Please allow me to trace what your eyes tell me."

I nodded, allowing him to lead me to the bed. I looked down at his fingers, interlocked with mine. These were the hands that had created so many world-renowned masterpieces. Although his grip felt rigid, his touch had become soft and tender.

I sank into the silk duvet as he rested on all fours above me. The back of his hand grazed the side of my face. He remained still, observing me before he caressed me again and whispered my name, as if to ensure it was I under him in the rapture of his arms. He then smiled and kissed me once more.

Continuing to stroke the side of my face, he closed in with another soft and warm kiss. He tasted like the wine from the gallery, which is when I realized what I had consumed hadn't been wine. It was some part of him that allowed others to see a different view of his world and his art. But it didn't matter. I was fully under his rapturous spell.

He raked my soft neck with his jaw. I began sucking on his chin and neck, including his bulging Adam's apple, all of which were roughened but soft. He took control once again with his lips and tongue, continuing to slide them around my neck and over my mouth. His muscular chest, solid beneath his dark clothes, pressed over mine. His loins and legs, including his muscled thighs, did the same. Our crotches ground together, mine firm and warm, his a large, rigid shaft.

His open black coat swallowed me up, while the bulges in our slacks continued to scrape and press against one another.

With both hands, he tore open my shirt and slid it off along with my coat. He removed my slacks and underwear, too, until I was naked for him under the soft light.

He stood up and watched me, studied my flesh in a way that made me aware of my nakedness. For the first time, out of all the times that I have lain naked, in full view for someone, I truly knew how it felt to be naked. He smiled at my lean, toned body with its hairless chest. Gracefully, he slid the tips of his fingers over my chest and navel.

He removed his coat and black shirt, exposing his wonderfully chiseled chest and the touch of raven-black hair on his pecs and pink nipples. The bulge crammed into his black fitted slacks was hefty, and his rounded biceps and forearms seemed soft.

He grazed over my neck with his thick pink lips, warming my throat and catering to it in a way I never before knew. He bit gently into the flesh of my neck, heating my blood into a frenzy. My penis, too, burned with desire for him and his secret flesh. Oddly, my neck somehow desired him most.

Slowly, he graced my neck with his lips and began sucking on it. I could even make out the tips of his teeth. I moaned for more. The thought of him stopping became so utterly unbearable that I found myself pressing my neck against his mouth up into his sharp incisors. I yearned for him to puncture me deeply so that I could submit to the ecstasy of being tasted.

I, too, wanted to taste the same red lava that makes a masculine being so alive. It was the way he worked on my neck, I was certain of it. My neck craved a climax only my cock could deliver. I moaned, sucking at his naked chest and nipples. I wrapped my hands over his soft back. I had never before known I could experience or indulge in a climax without climax.

My heart felt eternally his, pumping under his control, so that every cell whispered his name over and over: "Michael... Michael...Michael."

He moaned in ecstasy and whispered in my ear, "You are everything and yet more than I remembered, Adam. I can taste your secrets and desires, all of you. You are *my* Adam, forbidden fruit even as a mundane mortal being."

His moans continued. All I could grasp, while feeling such climax and frenzy, was my vertigo.

I had become lost in desire—drained as any orgasm tires the mind, only ten times more exhausting. I knew nothing more. I lay there for him to do as he pleased. Touch me or murder me—I did not care.

I shut my eyes. He continued to touch me, as if in a distant, dark dream. I smelled the tang of oil paints and heard the sound of a bristling brush daubing a canvas like a gentle lullaby that sang to me and of me.

As if in a dream, I could vaguely make out the colors of a new painting he created—clouds, wings, and fangs that broke into the skin of a masculine Adam's apple.

SCARECROW

Chris always took the same trail every morning when he jogged over the narrow path of foliage that extended beyond the grassy meadow slope. He had watched the wild grass become a pale gold, with fringes that stretched long enough to be confused for bundles of wheat. The scent of fall filled his lungs and the shifting colors introduced something new.

He'd been in Kansas since he graduated from art school in the spring, staying at his Aunt Edna's house. He wanted to get back to Chicago, jump-start his creative side by hitting the ad agencies, and move on after Sean. For the past four years, he'd known nothing other than the arts and the ex. Now, he wanted nothing more than to be in nature, paint, and sketch the summer in evergreen trees without bumping into Sean. He could revitalize himself as if he were a child again, visiting for the summer.

That morning, even though the trees were tied together in a mist too dense and frosty for jogging, Chris ventured past the moist expanse of autumn-colored hills, beyond the meadow, unwilling to allow any gloom to obstruct his daily jog.

He only did a moderate run so he could enjoy the abundance of the various vineyards spilling over the fields and surrounding hills. Very little about the area had changed over the years. That's why the limp, distant shape stood out, perched over the orchards. It appeared crucified and dead, but it also represented the true arrival of fall.

Chris couldn't help but slow down, reducing his pace to a near halt, before he began heading toward the scarecrow. He jogged up the hillside to where the vineyard became moist. He trudged into it, trying to avoid the vines and wilted branches, including one twig that scratched at his leg like a long, slender fingernail.

The instant he approached, Chris could see how it had been fastened from its lower back. It hunched forward, its sagging legs and hands leaning lifelessly away from the old and rusted wrought iron crucifix. It wore stained and distressed denim trousers and a long-sleeved plaid shirt. A pair of gloves had been stuffed and sewn as hands, with rubber boots for feet, and a rounded head constructed from some sort of old linen cloak. As if this wasn't enough to scare the crows, a rubber mask had been cut and sewn over the front of the face, although Chris couldn't immediately see this because of the way its head slanted downward, obstructed by a short, rugged, brown hat.

Chris had to grin at the meticulous construction of such a lifelike figure. People must have time on their hands near the outskirts of Kansas, unlike in Chicago. He reached for the mask. When he adjusted it for a better look at the face, he stepped back in panic. A dead field mouse stuck out of the mask's mouth. The tail drooped from its lips, as if the scarecrow had feasted on it. Traces of dried blood had skidded down its mouth, toward its warped chin.

Chris winced in disgust. He stooped and dug his fingers into the dewy grass, wiping them frantically. The mouse must have gotten into the scarecrow's mouth, where it became trapped and died. The splattered blood, however, appeared too malicious. Chris had to observe the face one more time. But when he looked up, the scarecrow was already peering into Chris's eyes. Its profile had twisted, perhaps from his touching it.

Not only had the mask been sewn as a face, but its audacious creator even had the morbid imagination to embed glass marbles into its otherwise vacant sockets.

Chris was aghast by such impudence, one that targeted not only crows but *anyone* crossing its path, like Chris.

Slowly, he retreated to his trail and resumed his morning jog.

❖

That evening, after a long day spent lounging on the portico beneath the mansard roof of his aunt's French cottage, Chris idly sketched the plain field that gave way to the distant trees and sunset colors. Chris found himself thinking suddenly about the scarecrow. Specifically, he thought of how it was no longer there when he'd returned from his jog. It seemed that someone, perhaps its owner, had removed it. Most likely, they took it down to get the mouse out of its mouth.

Chris had become so lost in thought, the sudden screeching of the screen door startled him.

"Chris, honey, I didn't mean to scare you."

"That's okay, Aunt Edna."

"I just wanted to bring you some lemonade before dinner. You seemed so deeply absorbed in your work—which, by the way, is looking marvelous."

"Thanks, Aunt Edna. Hey, can you tell me who lives in the fields beyond that hillside? Is it still Old Mister Forester?"

"Oh, no, honey. That goes to show how long it's been since you've visited. Old Forester died some eight years ago. Apparently, he died right in his field from a heart attack."

"Didn't he ever marry anyone?"

"Uh-uh. I guess you can say he was on your team." Edna smiled, handing Chris the chilled glass. "He had a young man live with him once. This was way before your time. And that was quite tragic. Probably the most tragic thing that ever happened to Mister Forester."

"Was it his lover?"

"'Companion' is what we called it back then. Your mother and I thought his young male friend was just the most handsome man we'd ever seen. She hadn't married your father yet, of course. We suspected, but things like that were just left unspoken."

"What happened to the young guy?"

"Well, times were different. As you may imagine, those small-minded bigots didn't take kindly to that kind of behavior. One night, I remember your grandfather locked all the windows and doors and turned off every light in the house, as if to suggest we weren't home. I guess you could say he didn't want to be involved."

"Involved?"

"Yes. I remember your mom and I went to peek through our bedroom window after hearing distant voices in the hills. Your grandfather became furious, telling us to get right into bed. Honestly, we didn't know what was happening. We figured it was just silly grown-up stuff. Well, it turned out a group of local men forced themselves right into Forester's property, pulling that young man out of the house."

"What did they do to the guy?"

"It was just horrific."

"Did they beat him?"

"Oh, honey, they dragged his body across the field, kicking him and beating him without mercy until they killed him. As if that wasn't enough, they tied his body to the wooden slings on the field as if he were a scarecrow, claiming such a homosexual sinner would scare any black crow away. Oh, the poor thing…"

"What about Mister Forester?"

"Well, they beat him to a bloody pulp, but they didn't kill him. They say that's how he got his stutter. Poor man was never the same. The men assumed he would fear for his life, and leave town."

"But he didn't?"

"That's right. And good for him. As a matter of fact, he even attempted to hold a special service and vigil for his dead companion, but the church wouldn't allow it."

"What about the punishment for this crime? Did the men ever serve time for the murder?"

"Oh, honey, the whole cowardly act was overlooked, and not only by the church but by the law. Forester never said who the men were. He claimed he didn't get a good view of their faces with all the beating. Besides, no one would really listen to Forester, the poor man. But Forester had his own plans to avenge his lover's death. Within a year's time, all of the men died in some tragic way. As much as each of their deaths appeared to be accidents, and therefore no fingers could be pointed, all of their deaths occurred much too close together. It made people wonder if Forester was murdering each one of them."

"Wow, I never imagined that of Old Mister Forester. No wonder my childhood impression of him was that he kept to himself."

"Always did. He was a generous man nonetheless, always so giving. Incidentally, as a result of the church's lack of concern, people say Forester held a service all on his own and buried his lover's body right in his field, where the corpse had been staked like a scarecrow. Funny thing is, after that, his harvests in that field tripled. They say even rodents would keep away."

"You mean as if a scarecrow was actually there?"

"Exactly."

Chris nodded, remembering the scarecrow in the fields, including the rodent. "Who lives out there now?"

"No one. Even Forester's house is gone. It was dismantled by some of his relatives who claimed they were going to rebuild a cottage and sell the entire lot, but I guess that plan just died in the works. The field is the only thing left of Forester."

"There was a scarecrow in those fields this morning," said Chris. "Funny thing is, on my way back from my jog, it was gone."

"That doesn't seem right. Are you sure?"

"Honest to goodness."

"Hm." Edna shrugged. "It's best you keep away from that hillside."

"Why?"

"Don't mean to scare you from your morning routine, Chris, but people say Forester went sort of crazy after that tragedy."

"What does it matter? He's dead."

"His craziness was a result of the tragedy. You see, after his lover's death, Forester posted in his fields a scarecrow that oddly resembled him. That hideous thing even wore some of his lover's clothes. The way that scarecrow dangled on that crossbar was creepy. It even had a rubber mask sewn on its face that looked like his lover. Some people claimed Forester dug up his boyfriend's body simply to mold a mask that would resemble his face. People didn't know what to make of it. It was like he erected it to protect his territory—not from crows but from people. Or remind them of what they had done."

"Oh, c'mon, Aunt Edna. I saw that hideous thing. What? You think that scarecrow is gonna jump me or something?" Chris laughed, as if the scarecrow had never unnerved him.

"Chris, don't you go near that scarecrow. It's best you leave it alone. Promise me that."

Chris leaned forward over his stool, as if to catch her attention, then stepped inside the house. "Aunt Edna, what was the companion's name?"

At first, she remained still. "His name was Sean," she said, before regaining her usual smile. "But don't worry, dear. He looked nothing like your ex-boyfriend."

❖

That night, Chris dreamed of Sean, but not of his ex. In his dream, Sean was young and handsome, with eyes that were a golden-honey brown. Chris saw him working out in the field, shirtless and chiseled, his skin moist under the soft golden rays of the sun.

Chris jogged through the dreamscape hillside, admiring Sean from a distance until *it* appeared again. Then Sean was no longer plowing the field, but hanged like some crucifix. His face and body were dismantled and bloodied. And just as Chris closed in on Sean, a decomposing rat with a long tail swung lifelessly from its mouth. The grim nightmare startled Chris. Awakening, Chris found his room still dark, the menacing sound of crickets stirring outside his window.

Chris sat up, facing the open window as he thought about the companion, Sean. The bulbous moon peeked partially into the window frame.

His dream had felt so real, he needed to breathe the night air to forget it. But even as he stood up and walked over to the unscreened window, thoughts of the horror that unfolded for Sean and Forester seized him.

Outside, the nearby trees and distant hillside were faintly illuminated under the moonlight with a hint of fog. Chris leaned against the window ledge. Ahead, the trees separated enough to permit a partial view of the hillside, then gave way to a wooded area that led to old Forester's fields. He pictured the murderous men, with their flashlights and picks, heading over that hillside the night of their homicidal rampage. He also pictured himself heroically intervening and fighting those stupid men, defending poor Sean.

Would he have done that if he'd been there? Times were different, after all, as his aunt had put it, and Chris was not the confrontational type. He'd run away from his ex. The thought disgusted him, and he looked around his monastic attic room. Why was he still at his aunt's house, way past summer?

He felt as though the trees watched him watching them. That's when he sensed something oddly out of place. He looked again and saw the scarecrow staked on his aunt's lawn, sagging lifelessly just like Chris remembered. Chris jerked back in fear, nearly falling to the floor. How could it be there, only a few feet beneath his safe haven?

Was the scarecrow alive? Could it see Chris? As if under the scarecrow's spell, Chris slowly went to the window, where it presented itself again, causing a chill to run down Chris's back.

This time, Chris slammed the window shut, closed the curtains, and bolted from the room.

He knocked on his aunt's bedroom door before cautiously opening it. "Aunt Edna? Aunt Edna…you there? You awake?"

No answer.

Chris turned on the lights, finding only crumpled blankets over the empty mattress, indicating she had slept in them earlier.

"Aunt Edna!" Chris shouted.

He heard a rustling sound from outside Edna's window, which faced the same part of the yard where the scarecrow had been staked. Chris gazed at the window, seeing a sloped shadow against the white curtain. It extended outward and wore a skewed hat. It seemed to be watching Chris through the sheer curtain panel, elongating its crucified shape into Edna's room. That's when the dreadful possibility dawned on him.

He rushed out into the dark corridor, stumbling as he called for her. "Aunt Edna!" He turned on more lights and lamps. "Aunt Edna?" His voice trembled.

Silence.

Chris remained still, listening and watching for any sign of his aunt. Just as he prepared to shout out her name once again, the rustling sound came louder from the exterior of the house, followed by a harsh thumping.

Chris's eyes widened in fear. He was certain the sounds were coming from outside, near his aunt's bedroom. He went back into her room. The wind blew the curtain in, revealing dark horizons of trees. He searched for the shadow of the scarecrow, but it was nowhere to be seen.

He went to the window and yanked aside the curtains, but when he looked out into the yard, he saw no sign of the scarecrow.

Taking a deep breath, Chris faced the hallway. As much as fear had weakened him, he was starting to get mad. "This is ridiculous! I'm not gonna be victim to some asshole's joke."

With speed and fury, Chris went through the house and unbolted the front door. When he flung it open, the silhouette presented itself smack in front of him—just a few feet below the porch steps. The scarecrow faced him directly, its limp body hanging on the cross, its marble eyes gleaming under the moonlight. Chris couldn't believe his eyes. Somehow, the thing had gotten to the very front of the house.

Slowly, Chris walked up to the lifeless scarecrow and grabbed its legs, wrestling it toward himself. "Oh, yeah? Think this is funny? Fuck you, assholes!"

With all his strength, Chris seized the scarecrow and trudged toward the forest. When he reached its dense trees, he grunted and brutishly tossed it several feet ahead, where it slammed into the dirt and dry leaves, and was quickly cloaked in the hazy fog. "There you go, fucker! Let's see if you can get up again."

Chris let out a deep breath and jogged back to the house.

All the lights were out.

Chris's knees began to buckle. As much as he attempted to avoid any inane conclusions, he couldn't help but feel his throat thicken with fear. Cautiously, he stepped inside the house, turning on the living room lights. The room remained empty with still no sign of his aunt. He called out for her before going back to her bedroom. This time, the light switch did not work.

A harsh pounding from the front door startled him, and he whipped around.

"Aunt Edna!" he shouted, rushing toward the living room. "Aunt Edna! God dammit!" As he reached for the doorknob, the pounding stopped. Somehow, he found enough strength to fling the door open.

Again, all he could see was the sparse trees and field.

"Aunt Edna?" he whispered.

He stepped out onto the porch, every plank of wood creaking under him. Creeping toward the distant trees, he looked everywhere for any sign of his aunt.

"Where the hell is she? God dammit—Aunt Edna!"

At first, he thought it was a cluster of thickened haze and fog that did not dissipate as easily as the rest. But it was the scarecrow dead ahead. Its eyes gleamed in the dark, watching Chris.

Chris bolted toward the house, his heart pounding as if it were going to burst from his chest. And just as he was approaching the porch, he managed to gather enough courage to look behind him. To his horror, the scarecrow was moving rapidly in his direction! The ghostly being, with its flannel shirt and contorted mask, ran swiftly behind Chris, its marbled eyes glinting.

Chris screamed, stumbling onto the front porch after missing a step. His shoulders collapsed first, falling against the wooden deck. Next, a sharp throbbing pain came from his knee when he hit the staircase edge.

The scarecrow continued advancing on Chris. Its features were no longer of soft plastic but of *true* flesh. Its piercing wide eyes blazed pale gray in the moonlight. No more were they marbles. The scarecrow had become human and real.

Chris twisted onto his back before curling into a protective fetal position. The pain shot through him everywhere.

He attempted to ignore it and picked himself up off the porch by supporting his weight on his elbows. He focused on the scarecrow's face, seeing gruesome bruises and bloodied scars.

Chris couldn't look away. Desperation filled the scarecrow's face, but Chris saw youth beneath the horror—a face which once belonged to a handsome young man.

Chris's body froze. It was *Sean* returning from the grave, avenging his own death. And Chris was his next target. But why? Chris had sympathized with Sean and Forester. Chris had even dreamed of avenging Sean—of killing Sean's killers.

"Chris!" Someone's desperate call echoed from deep within the woods. Aunt Edna. "Chris!"

Her cries became louder, echoing against the trees, until she appeared and spotted him. "Chris!"

His aunt came rushing in his direction, carrying the scarecrow he'd tossed in the forest.

"Chris!" Edna shouted desperately as she stopped, facing Chris and Sean. With both hands, she jabbed the sharp iron cross bearing the dangling scarecrow into the ground. "Leave him alone!" Edna shouted to the zombie-like creature.

Chris gazed into Sean's eyes, which continued to reflect rage, until Sean saw the lifeless scarecrow Aunt Edna had brought with her. Sean's eyes widened in fear and repulsion at the limp replica of himself—Sean.

To Chris's amazement, Sean began to dissolve, his face the first to go, until he had fully vanished and only Chris and his aunt remained, catching their breath.

"Are you okay?" asked Edna, still clutching the perched scarecrow.

Chris sat up and faced his aunt, who was kneeling before him, her hands reaching for his back.

"I don't know!" Chris answered. "How about you? What just happened?"

"I'm fine," said Edna, nodding. "It keeps him away. That's why old Forester used to place that scarecrow in the fields! To keep *Sean* away!"

"You mean his lover?"

"Yes," she answered. "Forester knew Sean was avenging his own death, and he created that scarecrow to keep Sean from returning. So that scarecrow must always be protruding from the ground. If it's not up and visible, then Sean returns.

Every fall. We all take turns moving it around. That's why I brought it close to my house. It is our turn to place it on our lawn. I kept moving him tonight because I knew the spirit of Sean was lurking around our house."

"Why couldn't you have told me?" Chris curled his hands and fingers with anger. "Besides, I don't understand. You disappeared, Aunt Edna..."

"I was only partially hiding because I didn't want to explain my reason for having the scarecrow on our lawn. When I saw you turn the light on in my room, I knew you were awake, so I moved him to the front, hoping you would go back to bed. I never imagined you would step out of the house, or worse, that you would throw it into the woods. That's when I rushed to find him. I knew he would come looking for you."

"You should have told me."

"I didn't want to tell you," said Edna. "You were just visiting for the summer. I was hoping you wouldn't have to find out—especially not this way."

Chris didn't respond. Instead, he looked at scarecrow Sean, its mask devoid of the bruises and scars the real Sean had endured.

❖

The next morning, Chris packed up and prepared to return to the big city. He no longer wanted to pretend he was a hero defending Sean and Forester. Instead, he wanted to prove to himself that he could, at the very least, face life on his own without *his* Sean, just like Forester had done.

Cirque des Freaks

W hat do you think? Freaky?" asked Chelsea with a smile.

"Definitely," Gifford said, pressing his lips together tightly as he nodded. "I mean, *Jesus*, if that bald midget coils that whip around himself any more, he'll look like one of those child mummies we saw at the Louvre."

The two of them laughed heedlessly, their faces close and hidden from the rest of the circus spectators. Gifford tossed Chelsea's wavy red hair behind her shoulders.

Robbie did not look at all amused by their behavior. She squinted viciously, creasing her brown skin, and shook her head, but her hair remained a stiff shrub without sway.

Chelsea curved her hand over her mouth in an attempt to restrain her laughter, but it was too late. Already she had spewed a gust of giggles aimed mistakenly at her girlfriend Robbie.

With wide, condemning eyes, Robbie gestured with an index finger to her lips for the two of them to be silent. "*Mon Dieu!* You guys are being extremely rude. You're embarrassing me. *Fermez les bouches!*"

"Robbie, *mon amie*," Gifford said. "Don't be so brutal. We're here to laugh. Isn't that what the circus is all about? *C'est jolie, oui?*"

"Please, you guys have been laughing at the expense of this poor midget the instant he came out. And this is not supposed to be a comical skit."

Perhaps it was Robbie's seriousness or the severity of her tone, but either way, Chelsea and Gifford burst out laughing once again, this time distracting those sitting around them on the bleachers.

"Shhh!" Robbie hissed.

"All right, all right, we'll cut it out, baby," said Chelsea, leaning forward and kissing Robbie briefly on the lips. "It's Gifford. He always makes me laugh!"

"Yeah, I forget how you get when your best friend from New York comes to visit us in Paris."

"*Parce qu'il est mon chère*," said Chelsea, smiling. "He is my puppy dog, after all, and everything is catch-up time for us from our good ole days in New York."

"Okay, but please, baby," said Robbie, "let's enjoy the show first. That means you, too, Tootsie Doll." Robbie winked at Gifford.

Silently, the three of them watched the midget and contortionist act. And this time, Gifford and Chelsea would not so much as look at each other for fear of losing themselves hysterically.

Gifford leaned back, noticing how mostly families and couples crowded the bleachers. There wasn't much that appealed to him about the act, not even the slender clown on stilts, flame gushing from his reddened mouth.

An elderly heavyset woman wearing a baby jumpsuit and an oversized bib rode a tricycle in circles while a mime imitated her and two other clowns chased her.

He glanced over at Chelsea, whose hands rested in her girlfriend's lap. He couldn't recall the last time Chelsea had looked so content and at peace. She'd left him behind in the Big Apple, but she'd managed to meet a Parisian who could give her a home in a wonderful place. Somehow, despite the countless artists and lipstick girlfriends, rock and roll boyfriends and Quaaludes in Chelsea's past, including her vegan years, living in Paris with a fierce liaison to the United Nations suited her. And now, he was able to visit her in Paris whenever he so desired.

He looked down at his Movado watch, wondering how much longer he would have to sit through the remaining acts, when the entire tent suddenly turned dark, dissolving the cheers and applause from the crowd.

Darkness continued for a couple of minutes before a fire pit in the center flashed harsh and tall flames, and an adjacent spotlight shone down on a tall man in a dark top hat. He was slender, a spectre in a black suit and matching cape of thick silk. The man stood motionless and silent, eyes cast on the crowd around him. A finely trimmed and slender black goatee surrounded his mouth, enhancing his pale skin and wide, dark eyes.

For a moment, it seemed only his eyes moved, scanning the crowd as if to ensure it was big enough for him to begin. He grinned, apparently pleased with what he had seen.

"*Bon nuit*...good night, *madame et messieurs*...ladies and gentlemen..." His voice was deep, almost raspy. "*Je m'appelle* Renault. I am your host. Now that you've seen *le normal du cette cirque*, we now present to you, *permettez-moi*, what we're really all about. *Ce n'est pas un cirque normal, mais c'est un cirque des freaks. Voil*à!"

Following Renault's words, a gush of heavy fog and a burst of blue flashing lights erupted where the fire had been. A woman appeared with a thick slithering snake coiling around her waist and naked cream-colored shoulders. Her soft, curvaceous body was almost entirely bare except for her leopard bikini top and short matching silk skirt. Her long, wavy, raven-black hair followed as she swerved her hips to the pace and rhythm of the castanets she played. She smiled, revealing frightfully pointy fangs, as if she were a vampire.

The snake continued to wrap around her waist, maneuvering its way up her chest and around her neck. In that instant, the snake reared its head above her, bared its vicious fangs, and plunged them into her neck. Blood erupted, trickling like lava between her breasts.

Screams and hollers came from the crowd, including Chelsea, but the dancing woman ignored them all. Instead, she moaned as if utterly indulging the wounds inflicted by the reptile.

Two more snakes slithered toward her from out of the dark, each encircling a leg as they twisted upward. The two of them met the third one, their mouths also seeking her neck. Soon, all three of them shared her.

The woman reached for one of them, embracing it almost perversely before bringing it to her own small fangs. She bit it near the head, sucking at it while the other two snakes joined her. And when she had had enough of the wounded snake, she tossed it aside while the two other snakes still clung to it.

"Ladies and gentlemen!" Renault's voice filled the canvas enclosure. "*La femme fatale!*"

The woman faced the crowd with her mouth open, exposing her fangs and the snake's smeared blood.

Out of the pervasive fog behind her emerged the silhouette of a man. Only his legs and chest were visible at first, then both of his heads came into sight. Both faces had the same animated smile, each of them acknowledging the crowd around it.

More beings surfaced from the fog, including a man with an oversized bald head and hands that resembled the feet of a Gila monster, and a woman in a blue pastel tutu who spun with her hands curved above her head until she left the ground. She came back to earth, turning to show the crowd the small wings on her back. Also, the midget had returned, this time holding hands with an overly slender woman twice his height who possessed a coarse, dark beard that had grown past her chest.

Renault raised his arms, and the torches encircling the floor flamed up. He searched the crowd on the bleachers, stopping at Chelsea, Gifford, and Robbie.

"*Ouu la, cette un ménage a trois, oui*," he said with a smile, "but I only need one of you."

"No," said Gifford. "There's no *ménage a trois* here! They're lesbos, I'm a fag!" he laughed.

Renault's left eyebrow rose, and he slanted his mouth curiously. "The soul knows not of such sexual boundaries, *monsieur*. You have much to learn."

Gifford didn't respond. Instead, his eyes became fixed on the man's sleek white skin and sharp, slender nose. Gifford wasn't sure what it was, but everything about Renault's presence seemed inescapable, as if it had the evil capacity to haunt him forever.

"I shall tell you, *monsieur*, and all my other circus guests today, I shall prove to you—especially you, Gifford—that every living thing is easily opened and always willing to step beyond its boundaries of this world."

Gifford swallowed nervously, wondering how the ringmaster knew his name. "How so?"

"With this redheaded beauty!" he said, lifting his hand toward Chelsea. "That is, if she will allow me the honor of demonstrating this to her!"

Chelsea smiled. "I think you need to ask Robbie, my girlfriend, for permission."

Robbie slanted her head in disapproval. "If you want to prove that someone can step beyond their boundaries, then you've got the wrong girl. It's this one, Miss Frigid-and-Single over here," she said, pointing at Gifford, "who can give you a run for your money."

Some of the crowd snickered, but there was an overall applause of encouragement for proof.

"Ah, a comedian," said Renault. "Actually, I can assure you your girl has never crossed *these* boundaries. But if she allows it, she may even enjoy it."

"Fine by me." Robbie's eyes rolled in exasperation.

Chelsea simpered as she rested her hand over Renault's open palm before he led her into the circus ring. When she reached the center, all the entertainers encircled her.

Chelsea glanced at the gruesome ensemble, which included the double-headed man standing only a few feet away from her. His four eyes observed her curiously, just as all the other so-called freaks ogled and leered at her.

Chelsea could feel all the hairs on her body stand as a chill ran through her.

As if the freaks' presence wasn't enough, she stiffened instantly at the crack of Renault's whip, which demanded everyone's attention.

"Ladies and gentlemen, prepare to watch this beauty join our world, as she becomes one of us."

Slowly, the ensemble encircled her even closer, walking around her, approaching her face with every step. She could feel the warmth of their breath on her face and neck, causing her skin to prickle with goose bumps.

Chelsea could feel her heart race with pure panic. As much as she tried not to look at the bearded woman, the uncanny double-headed man, the woman with wings, and the near nude *femme fatale* with a snake around her neck, not to mention the midget, her eyes were magnetized to the aberrations before her. And when they stopped moving, standing as close as they could get, she faced the woman with the snake.

A beat of drums began to thump loudly from the same distant quartet that had been playing throughout the show.

The beauty facing Chelsea began to dance again, as her snake slithered southward. Chelsea trembled.

"Do not be alarmed, *madame*," said Renault, standing close by. With an abrupt snap of his whip, a large cloak of burgundy silk materialized out of nowhere. He flung the sheet into the air so that it landed over the circle of freaks, concealing the entire ensemble, including Chelsea.

Almost immediately, the crowd sensed an indistinguishable stirring beneath the burgundy mantle, which enshrouded whatever frightful magic was occurring. The crowd hollered and even screamed fitfully.

"Hey!" Gifford cried, as Robbie squawked.

Waves rippled the surface of the burgundy silk as if such commotion defined some struggling, fighting, and even pain. To everyone's shock, the sheet suddenly dropped and crumpled flatly on the floor, with no shape or sign of anyone under it at all.

The crowd cheered and clapped in frenzied amazement.

Soon, something began to stir beneath it. It swerved and slithered under the burgundy silk until the snake peered out and slithered toward Renault, its fangs dripping blood. Renault waited for the snake to coil around his leg and travel up to his shoulders.

"Did you have a good meal?" Renault asked.

"Where are they?" someone from the crowd shouted.

Renault smiled, watching as the cloak casually began to rise, a curvature swelling the silk. Renault cracked his whip once more and pulled the sheet away. Chelsea lay beneath it, flat on the floor of the ring for a breathless moment, before she slowly sat up.

Renault approached her, taking her hand and guiding her to her feet. "Ladies and gentlemen, I present to you a woman who has now traveled beyond the boundary and has tasted and seen my world."

As the crowd cheered and hooted, Robbie and Gifford each let out a deep breath of relief.

❖

The cool night brought a full, bulbous moon over Paris, including its tall, pointy Eiffel Tower. Night was alive with voices, and breezes that occasionally brought with them scents of some enticing dessert or coffee from the cafés of the Latin Quarter, where Chelsea, Gifford, and Robbie shared a bottle of wine at a small restaurant bar.

"So you don't remember a single thing?" asked Gifford, as he held his glass of red closely to his lips.

"Not a thing. The last thing I remember was feeling as though I was going to pee right there in the ring out of fear that those freaks were going to do something unimaginable! They were really scary, especially that two-headed man. I couldn't bear looking at him or those two heads any longer. They each moved with a life of their own."

"What about all that movement under the sheet, baby?" asked Robbie.

"I don't remember." Chelsea sipped her wine. "Now, this may sound weird, but all I can honestly bring back with me from that experience is a certain taste."

"A taste?" Gifford prompted. "What kind of a taste?"

"Uhm. I don't know. But if I could define what *black* tastes like, that would pretty much describe it."

"Black?" said Robbie. "I don't know. I'm still worried about you, honey."

"Actually, that taste still lingers. It's weird, but I even feel it in my chest, you guys. It's almost like blood, but black blood, like if one could taste old blood, that's what it would taste like."

"Honey, I don't think blood is what you're tasting," said Gifford. "I think the wine has just gotten to you."

Gifford wasn't sure why, but something told him they hadn't seen the last of them, that the freaks were capable of returning. Maybe even coming back for Chelsea.

He forced himself to laugh, as if he had paid attention to whatever comment Robbie had just said that made Chelsea laugh.

That night, after heading to a gay bar on the Champs-Elysées, where the three of them joined some of Robbie's Parisian friends for more wine, Gifford was finally feeling more at ease with the whole circus incident.

The life of Paris had sneaked its way back into his heart, enough so that he had managed to almost forget the creepy carnival occurrence and truly feel as though love and enchantment still awaited.

❖

The three of them didn't return home until well past midnight. Robbie owned an apartment building near the Arc de Triomphe, where she lived with Chelsea. Gifford slept soundly in the vacant unit Robbie kept open for all of Chelsea's visitors. It was on the same floor as Robbie and Chelsea's unit. Gifford liked how its windows faced the city, its bold moldings defining its age and architectural splendor.

Distantly, he heard the echo of laughter. It was short, but loud enough that it awoke him. He sat up in bed, facing the small studio. The laughter was near. Someone was in the building, he was certain of it.

The sound of footfalls and whispers—someone wandering the hallway—had become louder and unmistakable. He made his way to the front door, hoping it was some tenant sharing the same floor.

He peeked into the peephole. The hallway—immediately in front of the door, at least—was empty. All he saw was a wall with damask wallpaper of gold and turquoise and a purple carpet runner below. The peephole view appeared compressed and magnified.

Gifford thought maybe he had imagined the laughing and moving sounds, since the hallway had become silent. But then he caught a glimpse of something familiar passing by quickly. It was tall and slender Renault with his top hat. As if that wasn't enough, Renault's entourage followed obediently behind: the bearded woman, the two-headed man, the man with Gila monster hands, the winged woman in a tutu, and the voluptuous female entangled with a slithering snake.

All of them were heading toward the end of the hallway, in the direction of Chelsea and Robbie's flat.

Gifford's heart began to race, especially when he blinked and saw the midget staring level with the peephole, grinning at Gifford. The reptile man had lifted the midget to face the peephole so that Gifford had to undeniably acknowledge their presence.

Gifford stepped back, feeling as though he was going to faint. He needed to catch his breath, so he headed toward the window. He wanted to turn on the light, but that would only confirm that he was inside, afraid and vulnerable!

Next, he heard Chelsea scream. He looked around wildly, reaching for the first thing he could grasp, which was his umbrella. Holding it up, he headed for the door and unbolted it before flinging it open.

Gifford rushed out, in pursuit of Robbie and Chelsea's flat.

Even before he reached their unit, he could eerily make out Robbie's squealing and groaning.

"They've taken her, Gifford!" Robbie shouted frantically. "The freaks! They've taken my baby! And they tied me to the bed! You must go get her now!"

At first Gifford remained still, as if absorbing Robbie's words, never mind the sight of the way her hands and legs stretched and fastened with rope along the bed poles. Before he knew it, he had darted out into the dark and desolate streets, still clutching his umbrella, desperately searching for Chelsea or one of the freaks. Voices echoed in the distant dark, including a low whimpering that sounded like Chelsea. Gifford used these subtle noises to lead him to Chelsea and the freaks.

Uncertain where he was or where the voices had led him, Gifford stopped. Treating the umbrella like a cane, he rested the metal tip against the cobblestone to balance himself. Coughing and heaving for air, he eventually caught his breath. Though he was no longer youthful and strong, he was not about to give up.

After a moment, he scanned the narrow Parisian street. As he distantly spotted the Eiffel Tower, he recognized the voices of the freaks and the echoes of Chelsea's whimpers. They were coming from one of the abruptly curving alleys where night became darker and even the moon became concealed.

Carefully, Gifford navigated his way between the two buildings. Chelsea's whimpers persisted, but he also heard a familiar laugh. It was Renault, standing at the end of the alley with the rest of his crowd. As for Chelsea, her body lay frail and weak in the arms of the double-headed man.

"Let her go," Gifford demanded, raising his umbrella as if it were a weapon.

Renault looked up at the umbrella and grinned, pacing toward Gifford. "And what, take you instead?"

"What do you want with her?"

"We showed her *our* world, the underworld, a place that doesn't lie. A place that helps you confront your worst fears. And as much as she feared it, she enjoyed it." Renault snickered. "In fact, she's going to confront her worst fears shortly. Very soon, she will start to transform into the creature or physical abomination she fears most." Renault laughed, glancing over at Chelsea's limp and unconscious body. "Best of all, she will become one of us, and join our *Cirque*, where *mademoiselle* will depend on me."

"Bullshit! She didn't want any of this," Gifford cursed him angrily. "You're all freaks!"

"Trust me, she enjoyed it. You didn't see what was under the sheets."

"*Oui, il adore notre cirque*," said the lady with the snake around her waist. Her laughter reverberated through the alley.

"Fine, then take me instead."

Renault took a step forward so that his face was next to Gifford's. Slowly, he caressed the side of Gifford's face. "Actually, the closer I see you, the more I can appreciate your beauty. I mean, you are an older man, but still distinguished. There's a certain glow to you that I admit is almost as beautiful as your friend's here."

"Then take me with you."

Renault continued to soothe the side of Gifford's face. "I can only imagine what's in your mind—those fears that haunted you from infancy." Renault grinned and nodded. "I don't make deals. However, you've intrigued me. I'll make an exception."

"Then let her go," Gifford demanded.

Renault looked at the double-headed freak. Without a word, he gestured to let her go.

Gently, the man placed Chelsea's body on the cobblestone.

Gifford could feel Renault's eyes return to him. Renault's thumb was firm as he abruptly pressed it under Gifford's chin, pulling Gifford's lips to his. Gifford could feel Renault's warm breath before they kissed. Gifford gave in, relishing something dark and surprisingly piquant. His shoulders loosened as he tasted Renault and continued to surrender to him.

Their lips still locked, he felt the heavy silk of Renault's cape. Darkness settled over both of them, and a childhood memory came to Gifford.

Somewhere near the old farm shed on the green plains of his parents' plantation in New Orleans, Gifford was playing on the long, green pasture when he spotted red chicken claws, several of them growing out of the dirt. They appeared like flowers, but instead they were something else. Perhaps it was voodoo or the devil himself planting them to protect or infest their property. Either way, Gifford never forgot. Those red talons made him despise chickens.

This was the vision that flashed over him until he could feel Renault's lips no more. As if awakening from a dreary, heavy sleep, Gifford's eyes opened fully. He felt weak. Darkness surrounded him, along with a faintly familiar face. It was Renault, who had taken him captive.

Renault grinned, still caressing the side of Gifford's face as his cape concealed their tightened bodies.

Despite Gifford's state of weariness and even his partial attraction to Renault, he knew the danger wasn't over. He focused on the handsome dark eyes, holding their attention. He knew what he needed to do. Still gripping his umbrella, Gifford secured his hold before shoving it upward between them with all his strength, piercing the metal tip deep into Renault's heart.

Renault's eyes widened, continuing to look directly at Gifford as blood began to trickle from his lips.

"Ah!" the *femme fatale* screamed.

Renault dropped to the floor, blood spurting from his chest and mouth.

Gifford reached for Chelsea and lifted her body into his arms. As she started to stir, returning to life, Gifford strode away, leaving Renault to die in the streets of Paris and the freaks to survive on their own.

❖

After making sure Chelsea was safe and back with Robbie, he caught the first flight back to New York, where he took a nightcap of whiskey to help him sleep through his flight. It seemed to work, until something shook him from slumber.

He had been dreaming of the old plantation and those grotesque chicken feet. His eyes ached and felt dry, perhaps from the stale cabin air. His feet itched, so he reached down to scratch them, then jerked back. He had jabbed something sharp below his knees. He looked at his hands, and to his horror he saw red.

His hands were like talons, with the three sharp claws of a chicken.

Gifford stumbled out of his seat and rushed into the restroom, locking himself into the little compartment. In the mirror he saw how black and elongated his eyes had become.

He was transforming into his worst nightmare, converting into one of those freaks. He had killed the one who would have been his master. He had orphaned the other freaks, including himself.

He tried to scream, but only a short, guttural cluck came out of his mouth.

RAZOR CUT

Three weeks and two days had passed, and Fidell still hadn't come in requesting Mateo for his usual cut and close shave with hot towel. It wasn't like Fidell, with two l's, to go beyond fourteen days without a haircut. Part of Fidell's routine was to sit silently vigilant in the chair, swallowing sparingly.

Mateo noticed and lusted over all of these minute details, including Fidell's suits and classic wingtip shoes. Most of all, he lusted for Fidell's ultra-pale skin that brought out his large, dark eyes, heavily framed by wings of the same raven hair that softly caressed his arms and wide knuckles.

He embodied streams of countless veins, hair thin to pulpous spaghetti, like the Vitruvian man—from those veiny roots in the white of his large eyes to the ones that slithered around his knuckles and neck, including his jugular vein. Ah, *yes*…that jugular vein, always restless under Mateo's blade, breathing with life at such close, vulnerable range.

Again, Mateo devoured all these details. Fidell wanted nothing to do with the others at the barbershop in the Downtown Arts District, where warehouses had long been a conversion of domestic hubs for urbanites.

So far, according to Mateo, the bond between the two had become something to remain hopeful about. What that could mean remained speculative, just like Fidell. Mateo waited like a servant to his master. That was true Mateo. That was the power of Fidell.

Mateo saw something dark and robust from the corner of his eye. Something familiar and tall watched. Again, he hadn't scheduled an appointment, but that was okay on this desolate, gloomy mid-morning. Mateo's scissors and razor were ready for Fidell. So was his heart.

"Perfect timing," said Mateo.

Fidell remained rigid and still, moving his eyes downward in the direction of the deep burgundy vinyl barber's chair Mateo was now pointing at.

"You see, I had a cancellation this morning," Mateo added. "Besides, it's been a bit slow. Please, sit down."

"You're all alone," Fidell finally said.

"Yeah, my partner is out getting his tattoo completed. Our other two barbers have become part-timers."

Without a word, Fidell sat.

"Will it be the usual?"

Fidell nodded, allowing Mateo to drape his body with the black apron so that only his polished black wingtip shoes peered out from underneath.

Adjusting his Wahl clippers to an eighth-inch-length guard, Mateo rolled up his white fitted sleeves, partially exposing the open scissors tattooed on his forearm. Mateo set the clippers down and reached for his scissors as he began to work his way in slow motions over Fidell's head.

"What was the insignia?" Fidell asked.

"You mean my business partner's tattoo?"

Fidell didn't respond.

"A cello," Mateo said with a smirk. "You wouldn't think it'd be such an ordeal, requiring so many sessions, but the graphic involves very complex colors and details."

Fidell said nothing.

"Yeah," Mateo mused, looking down at the ink on his own forearm. "I guess you could say this is my passion. Cutting and shaping hair is like an art to me. Both my father and grandfather were barbers."

He took a deep breath, the mirror reflecting a pensive Mateo and a deadpan Fidell.

"They're not around any longer, so I guess their tradition lives on through this barber shop my buddy and I opened some years ago."

Fidell's pupils appeared to enlarge. Then he shut his eyes and exhaled deeply with the touch of Mateo's fingers on his scalp.

Mateo began his cut. It was the art that he knew best, and it allowed him to become focused. He always felt comforted by the texture of so many fine filaments nesting into natural waves or flat and aligned against his slender fingers. He would work Fidell's hair this way before introducing the clippers.

All he heard in the little shop was the sound of his scissors and Fidell's breathing, keeping pace with his pulsing neck vein. Mateo watched the jugular with every escaping breath. Bold and imprinted with life.

Mateo knew Fidell's breathing pattern and wondered if the stoic, masculine beast under his fingers breathed the same way when making love. The thought of it made Mateo blush. Instead, he focused on the wisps of hair caressing his knuckles before floating to the floor. That's when Mateo curled a bundle of loose hair between the softness of his thumb and forefinger. Mateo looked down at the raven hairs he held and slid them into the large pocket of his apron for a personal keepsake.

❖

That late evening, before closing the shop, Mateo placed the thick strands into a small plastic bag that he then shoved into his messenger bag. He hopped on his bike and rushed through rows of warehouse-converted lofts until he reached Mission Road, where the distant view of downtown Los Angeles flickered and his studio apartment waited.

Barely having time to brush his teeth and change clothes, Mateo headed out again, this time on foot, to a tiny dive bar only blocks from his place, where he met up with friends. It became a late night of drinking one too many whiskies, and Mateo half-stumbled back to his apartment many hours later.

Back at home, he guzzled half a bottle of spritzer, then headed for bed. That's when he spotted his messenger bag. He had almost forgotten about the strands of hair, bundled and stashed for his private viewing.

He had no particular plan for Fidell's hair. It was simply his way of prolonging Fidell's presence. The more he thought about it, the more he felt ashamed and foolish. It was all new territory with a client.

Either way, he was buzzed and not only more forgiving of his own actions, but also able to take some pleasure in his souvenir, whatever that meant.

Pulling out the plastic sack, he saw the hair curled like a dark embryo. He drew out the contents, closing his eyes momentarily and feeling the texture before looking down again and noticing its intense darkness. Mateo swallowed. It was a piece of the man himself, and it was now in his open palm.

Inhaling deeply, he could taste the residue of the whiskey as his heart thudded softly. Studying his souvenir, he suddenly felt resentful. He had gone so far as to take the hair of a client, a man whom he found very attractive and by whom he was completely seduced, someone who hadn't been bold enough to reciprocate and actually ask Mateo out on a date.

Bringing the wisps under his nostrils, Mateo inhaled a faint scent of oil and musk while trying to recollect Fidell's features. Tenderly, he placed the hair back into its plastic pouch and into the top drawer of his nightstand.

That night he dreamed of dark skies and raven birds, but mostly of soft caresses over his face and neck by something soft and wispy, something that felt like Fidell's hair. It curled around his neck and worked its way around his lips before thrusting itself into his mouth, engulfing yet arousing Mateo, so that when he awoke, he grabbed his neck to make sure nothing was covering it. A vague, oily residue remained in his mouth.

❖

The next day, he thought of his dreams, but only briefly. Life at the barbershop had been a busy one without any sign of

Fidell, but Mateo knew he wouldn't be in. He would have to wait precisely fourteen days before Fidell would return. It was clockwork. But Mateo had become less disciplined. Something about the strands of hair made him feel more connected to and desperate for the tall and pale handsome figure.

"Hey, bro, are you okay?"

Mateo looked over at his business partner. "Huh?"

"I asked if you're okay."

"I'm fine."

"Are you sure? 'Cause you could have fooled me. We've had a full house today, and you've barely talked to any of our clients."

"I'm not much of a chatterbug," Mateo said.

"Well, you could have fooled me, 'cause that's usually not the case with you. To be honest, you seem sort of different."

"Different how?" Mateo asked.

"I don't know, just different. You're usually the one for small talk with everybody."

"And today I'm not?"

"Not only are you distant, but you look sorta different, man."

"How so?"

"I don't know. Your hair is, like, darker than usual. And you look pale white. Did you dye your hair? Even your forearms seem hairier or something. I don't know, man. I don't check you out to know exactly, but you just seem different."

Mateo didn't answer. Instead, he peered into the mirror over his empty station. He didn't feel different, but his business partner was right. There was something bolder about the look in his eyes. Indeed, his face seemed paler and his hair seemed darker, but he, too, wasn't sure why.

"Anyway, whatever, man. Just get some rest and be sure to lock up. I'll see you in the morning."

Again, Mateo didn't answer. In the mirror, his focus had shifted to the scissors tatted on his forearm, representing a generation of barbers. For a second, he thought he saw the visage of Fidell in lieu of his own, but he could never be Fidell—mysterious, bold, elusive.

Mateo walked home that night, beyond the Arts District and into the little desolate backstreets of downtown that were home to him. The neighborhood wasn't gentrified, so he still dodged the occasional homeless guy and tagged wall. Pacing through the 101 freeway underpass, Mateo rushed home thinking of his shameful addiction, increasing more with each passing night. Stealing Fidell's hair didn't bother him anymore. Now, it was his mounting fetish to embrace it, think about Fidell as he caressed it, at times bringing the strands up to his lips. He envisioned Fidell's body, imagining this multitude of hairs as a replica of all others, down to the very private ones.

It was only natural that his desire would intensify to a physical state necessitating direct interaction. This time, he slid under the sheets, the bundle put aside on the nightstand like a joint he'd prepared to enjoy. He plucked a single strand, bringing it over his bare chest so that the subtle strands of his own chest hairs intermingled with the follicle.

Next, he brought it to his lips, puckering them so that the moisture from his mouth would plaster it like a web to a spider's prey. He tasted the filament. It was the taste of Fidell. He remained this way, touching himself, thinking of Fidell and how some physical part of Fidell was wedged between his lips. Fidell fully belonged to him in that moment, not just a souvenir. His moans continued until the final climax.

Mateo let out a deep wail. Pain and pleasure like never before.

With one hand still curled around his throbbing but depleting hard-on, Mateo exhaled. A sensuous, exhilarating flame of emotions had just coursed through him in a way he couldn't recall ever feeling before. In that moment, he felt rejuvenated. But continued orgasms would need fresh demands and fetishes.

Somewhere between his enervation from ejaculation and his need for sleep, he became immobile with exhaustion. He couldn't muster up enough strength to clean himself or even remove the strand from his lips. Fidell's hair would have to remain until he woke up. For now, only sleep mattered.

Again, the skies were the color of bruised black, and so were the crows, whose blinking eyes were the only visible things in such a dark night. A silver crescent moon smiled at Mateo, naked as he was in those woods. Somewhere a stream gurgled. Next, he felt the caresses of soft hairs over his face— Fidell's familiar hairs. It soothed him, then aroused him. He awoke, aching at having to return to his world.

Looking up at the dark ceiling, he knew it was still night. Silence lingered. But something was off, interrupting his breathing. That's when he remembered Fidell's hair was still on his lips. Catching his breath, his eyes widened, and he tried to make sense of the elongated shadows in his room, sharpened by the light coming from the vintage lamp on his nightstand.

Somehow, Fidell still seemed present, but none of it mattered. Heat concentrated in his groin, the pleasure so fervent that he let out a deep moan. Looking down, he could see his dick was fully erect and moving rhythmically, as if it had a mind of its own. That's when he saw the unimaginable.

The dark, thick strand of Fidell's hair had encircled his hardened penis, jerking him as it held him captive. The single strand of hair coiled and controlled Mateo's cock, violating him into a frenzy.

He moaned in fear and reached forward to grab hold of his dick and the filament manipulating him, but its grasp tightened, spiraling into multiple rings, choking his flesh so that pleasure became pain.

"Fuck!" Mateo hollered. "Leave me the fuck alone!"

He dug at his flesh, trying to pluck the hair away, but it seemed useless. His erection depleted fully from fear, and that's when he ripped the living, feasting hair from his dick.

If that wasn't horrid enough, it dropped from his shaking fingers and slithered away with the other remaining pieces, like centipedes escaping into the nooks and crannies of his room. Mateo sat up instantly. His eyes widened, and he watched the worm-like fragments in terror. He knew each particle had a vicious, predestined plan for him. They would be back.

❖

The next day felt like a daze, as if nothing was truly real. But it *was* real, and every chatty customer or cancelled appointment reminded him of how exasperating work could sometimes be. It wasn't until his partner was gone for the day and Mateo was alone, preparing to close up, that he spotted a stiff figure outside watching him from the window. Fidell's stern face and eyes were a painted shadow from the retiring evening sun.

Mateo thought of ignoring Fidell. The doors were locked for the night, so he was safe for now. But he knew he would never be truly safe, so Mateo went to the glass door and unbolted the latch, bowing his head slightly to welcome Fidell.

Casually, Mateo made his way to his station for Fidell to follow.

Reaching for the black cloak, he shook it to remove any leftover hairs before swinging it fully open over the empty leather seat. Obediently, Fidell sat, allowing the cloak to drape over his body as Mateo fastened it securely around his neck.

Mateo began by mixing the white foamy menthol with his badger brush and other ingredients, including hints of sandalwood, a concoction conserved through generations of barbers in his family. He massaged this into Fidell's jaw and neck before preparing the hot cloth. When it was hot enough, Mateo distributed the heated terrycloth evenly over Fidell's face, leaving only Fidell's nose exposed.

After several minutes, the heat penetrated Fidell's face and softened his skin. Mateo placed the straight razor open over the counter, making sure the blade was shiny and new. Mateo then removed the towel and any residue on Fidell's face.

Fidell peered upward at Mateo, who began lathering shaving cream onto Fidell's neck. He shut his eyes at the touch of the foam and Mateo's fingers, as if utterly relaxed.

Mateo remained focused. Everything was like clockwork, until he grazed Fidell's hair inadvertently with the side of his hand when reaching for his wet cloth. Mateo instantly removed his hand, bringing it up to his face as he looked down at his finger, then at Fidell's hair. He wanted nothing to do with Fidell's hair.

As he returned his hand to Fidell's neck, he felt the hairs of Fidell's head tighten around his wrist, as if they had stretched and grown like vines, clinging onto anything reachable. Mateo's heart raced in fear as his knees became weak.

Fidell opened his eyes and honed in on Mateo.

Mateo was about to scream, but the hairs were no longer around his wrist. Everything seemed normal. Even Fidell appeared confused, as if unsure of what had distracted Mateo.

Mateo caught his breath. He seized the straight blade and clutched it closely to Fidell's neck. That's when he noticed the familiar serpentine-like movement of Fidell's jugular vein.

Mateo's blade moved closer. He could end it all right in that moment. His eyes widened as he contemplated the outcome. Sweat broke out on his forehead. Was he truly capable?

Fidell gazed up at Mateo, as if awaiting attention.

Then he grinned and opened his mouth, and Mateo saw something inside. A black ball of hair sprouted wings and suspicious eyes. The bird came out of Fidell's mouth and proceeded to watch Mateo, much like the vigilant ravens in his dream. It spread its wings and took flight, circling the shop. Fidell continued to grin with piercing eyes.

Mateo's hand shook as he held the razor steady over Fidell's jugular vein. "Leave me alone!" he shouted.

Fidell laughed—until Mateo forced the blade down. It sliced Fidell's thick vein, squirting and spraying blood all over Mateo's shaking hands. Fidell gagged, his eyes turning upward.

Mateo dropped the blade, bringing his open hands close to his face. They were drenched in blood. It scurried down his forearms, including the scissors tattoo, the spreading blood becoming vein-like, pulsing and slithering as it reached into Mateo's shirt. The streaks of blood were all becoming strands of hair, encircling Mateo's wrists and arms until they held him captive.

"You know, you really shouldn't take things that don't belong to you," Fidell said suddenly as he stood up, his open wound flowing with blood and strands of hair that covered Mateo's body.

Fidell's teeth gleamed as he reached for the straight blade, forcing Mateo into the barber chair. "It's time for your close shave. I promise to be gentle."

Fidell laughed, bringing the blade down slowly.

WAX ENTRAPMENT

Even though he'd grown up in L.A., Paul had never seen this hillside with historic homes and meticulously manicured lawns. Its peaceful, warm presence was breathtaking and removed from the rest of the city. He felt ashamed his two friends visiting from Atlanta knew about the obscure neighborhood vicinity known as Angelino Heights and *he* hadn't ever heard about it.

"These homes are truly gorgeous," said Frank, with a hint of his Filipino accent. His posture remained rigid while his hands moved. "I can't believe some of these Victorian homes are over a hundred years old."

"Actually, they're not only Victorian," said Eric, Frank's boyfriend and instigator of the sightseeing escapade. He'd read all about it on the internet. "Some of the architecture varies from Eastlake Victorian to Queen Anne and even Craftsman. What's interesting is that they were built during the height of the land boom, about the mid-1880s. And they chose this precise location so people could be close to work, which is downtown below. Many of the old silent film chase scenes and neighborhood scenes were filmed here. There even used to be a trolley that went straight to downtown in minutes."

"Aren't there any homes just like these in Atlanta?" Paul asked, half sarcastically. "Surely you guys didn't come all the way here to see historic homes."

"Also," Eric continued, glaring at Paul viciously, "these small, iron hitching posts with horse-shaped head tips in front of each lawn are where people used to tie their carriage horses. That alone should tell you just how old some of these homes are."

"Wow," said Frank. "That's cool."

"That *is* cool," Paul said, attempting to ridicule Frank's compliment. "Thank you so much, Mister Tour Guide. I feel so enriched with Angelino history. Now, how about we stop walking these streets and head over to West Hollywood for a brunch with mimosas?"

"Hey, hey, Paula," Eric chanted jokingly, "Frank and I are gonna drag you just a few more blocks to admire these wonderful homes. There will be plenty of time for boys and mimosas later."

"Hey, check out that one," Frank said, pointing. "The detail on that house is amazing!"

Paul and Eric looked up at the tall, angular, three-story home with mostly two-toned yellows, white moldings, and hints of brown.

"This definitely dates to before the turn of the last century," said Eric. "All its fine details are obviously original—from the fine garrets and turrets to the elaborate bracketing. This one has some nice spindles and columns around the porch. Above its bay windows is the iron roof cresting and mansard roof."

"Could you imagine living here?" Paul said. "People or tourists always gawking at your home? It must become annoying after a while."

Eric let out a deep breath, putting his arm over Paul's shoulders. "Homes like these, dear friend, are meant to be shared with the world. It would be selfish otherwise."

"Indeed, it would," said a tall, slender old man. He stood against a small, wispy tree along the edge of the lawn, a curved bough of stringy willow branches partially concealing his face. The man took a step forward, leaning on a dark, wooden cane. His face was pale and wrinkled with deep, sunken eyes. His white hair was sparse, and he wore a dark three-piece suit.

"Gregorio at your service, young men," he said. His voice was raspy and monotonous.

"Good morning, sir. My name is Paul, and these are my friends, Frank and Eric. I take it this is your home?"

"Most certainly."

"We didn't mean to intrude," said Paul. "I guess that's the price for having something so elaborate. People will always want to admire it."

Gregorio remained silent, moving only his eyes as he looked at them.

"Well, I guess we'll be moving along now," said Eric, already taking a step away from the house. "Sorry to have disturbed you."

"Actually," said the man, "as you were saying, tourists do love to gawk at our homes here, but only a lucky few get to admire them from the inside. Particularly *my* house, which has been here longer than any of the others."

Gregorio paused momentarily to cough and catch his breath. "And today, my home is open to you gentlemen for your viewing pleasure, which is something I haven't permitted in many decades. That is, if you gentlemen would accept my invitation."

The three of them remained silent, looking beyond the old man to the enormous house and its pastel yellow boards.

"We would love to," Frank said. "It would be an honor, sir. My partner Eric and I are here from Atlanta. This is our first time in L.A."

The man merely smiled. He turned and limped toward the porch, leaning heavily on his cane. "Please, follow me."

Curious, the three men followed him up to the front porch, which partially wrapped around the exterior of the house. Gregorio opened the front door and ushered them into a small foyer, then through to the living room.

The three of them were taken aback by the array of antique furniture and architectural aesthetics. The home was charmingly maintained and pristinely polished. The scent of wood seemed to exude from the furnishings, floors, detailed wall moldings, and private crevices. It was the house's very own personal scent.

But Paul smelled something else coming from upstairs. He wrinkled his nose.

"This is truly a beautiful home," said Frank.

"Yes," Eric added, "very impressive, even the furniture. Have you lived in this house a long time?"

"My whole life. More than ninety years."

"Is that wax that I smell?" asked Paul, sniffing around the stairway. "Coming from the second floor?"

"That, my friend, is the core of the house—the one I was referring to," said Gregorio. "Please, be my guest. And enjoy what is up there. I'm too old to climb those steps, so feel free to investigate without me."

Paul looked at the stairway, then back at Gregorio, who smiled widely. It was the first real emotion the man had expressed. Paul thought he was harmless enough. However, he was still uncertain about venturing upstairs.

Before he could react, Frank and Eric sprinted up the stairway. "Thanks so much!" Frank's voice bounced off the walls as he disappeared up to the second floor with Eric behind.

"Wait!" Paul ran up after them.

They reached a long corridor of hardwood flooring. The hall was lined with small Oriental rugs, bookshelves, framed artwork, and Tiffany lamps atop polished tables. Frank and Eric were outside a single, partially open door at the end of the hallway.

Frank stepped inside first.

For a moment, Paul thought they were in a room filled with people.

But the crowd consisted entirely of wax figures.

"Wow!" Eric enthused. "It's like a museum in here!"

Paul examined the large room, which seemed to encompass the entire second floor, serving as storage for life-sized pieces that must have belonged to a museum once. The countless wax statues resembled historical figures and fictional characters, including The Phantom of the Opera and Dracula. Many possessed their own stages, but some shared space.

"Check out Houdini," said Eric. "He looks so real, and so does the woman he's elevating under that sheet."

Paul glanced at the tableau only briefly. He wandered around, becoming lost in the labyrinth of wax figures.

Frank ventured about the room, winding through the staged statues until he came to a set of three men in Victorian outfits. They were seated at a table, feasting on an elaborate dinner arranged on silver platters. But what caught Frank's attention was the golden gaze of the handsome figure in the center.

Every minuscule detail about the man seemed real—from his dark, loosely knotted ponytail to the short, dark fur over his forearms. Although it seemed slightly dense for a human being, it was handsomely masculine and appealed to Frank. He also liked the short, dark chest hairs that curled out of the wax figure's partially unbuttoned Victorian white shirt.

Frank couldn't help but wonder if the man's legs and private area were sculpted with the same precision. He imagined a hefty, plump bulk crammed under the silk of the handsome figure's yellow pants. The thought of it made his blood warm, arousing him right on the spot.

That's when Frank felt it.

It was as if the wax figure *knew* what curiosity swelled in Frank's mind, as it proudly sat frozen and feasting at the elaborate dinner table.

Frank examined the yellow in the figure's eyes, the way his brown and gold pupils meshed and gleamed under the soft light. Its eyes seemed too real, gazing at Frank fiercely and unblinkingly.

Sweat sprouted from Frank's forehead as he stared at the figure. His level of concentration had become so intense that, before he knew it, the man smiled, gesturing with his hand for Frank to take a seat and join them.

Frank jerked back, shocked by the reality of the scenario. He expected to find himself in the old room with various wax figures, but he was astonished to find himself inside an elaborate dining room, with three real-live men and laughter from several centuries before his time.

He looked around, trying to find some sort of false element about his surroundings that would debunk the whole situation. But there was nothing false about any of it. Even the Victorian clothes Frank suddenly donned were just as real as his new environment.

As he prepared to scream, the man who had intrigued him stood up and spoke, his voice echoing with masculinity and tenderness. "Do not be alarmed. Please join us. My name is Verneus."

Frank didn't respond. Instead, he attempted to catch his breath, as his eyes widened in disbelief. "I...I...I don't understand."

"Just take a sip from this chalice," said Verneus calmly, raising the silver goblet in front of Frank.

Frank looked at the burgundy fluid inside, but before he could figure out what it was, Verneus was already tilting the chalice past Frank's lips.

Frank tasted a dry-bitter combination with the aftertaste of something putrid. His face shriveled as he prepared to spew it out, but suddenly everything around him began to swerve and swirl. He attempted to focus, but all he could make out was Verneus, the chalice, and the other two men. Only their presence mattered.

He sat down, preparing to partake of their meal. Frank watched the two men flanking Verneus eat ravenously, as if this meal would be their last. He found the way they gulped at their chalices, the red trickling down the sides of their face, uncivilized and disturbing.

Frank observed in wonder, detecting poultry on their plates and in their hands. From the corner of his eye, he could see Verneus watching him in amusement.

Verneus slid his plate toward him, encouraging him to eat. "Are you not hungry?"

"No, thank you."

"Very well," said Verneus, opening his palm for Frank's hand. "The night is beautiful, and the moon is ample. Please accept my invitation for a stroll under its radiance."

Frank looked into Verneus's hypnotic eyes of gold and brown and put his hand in Verneus's flat palm. He glanced over at the two men once more. Both of them grinned at him with food and wine on their teeth, their eyes wide.

Outside, Frank and Verneus walked hand in hand deep into the woods, the moon as ample as Verneus had described. Indeed, the full moon enhanced Verneus's golden eyes.

Suddenly, Verneus stopped and released Frank's hand. Stroking the side of Frank's face, Verneus opened his mouth and kissed Frank savagely. Frank felt Verneus's firm grip around his wrist, and he brought his hand up to Verneus's pecs, resting his palm above its soft, curled hair. Verneus ripped his shirt open and smiled proudly. Under the moonlight, his teeth gleamed like his silken yellow trousers. Verneus reached for Frank's hand once again, pressing it against and veering it along his body.

"I saw the look in your eyes," Verneus said with a smile. "I saw you wondering what I look like under these pants."

Frank swallowed as he felt Verneus's hirsute chest.

"Would you like me to show you?"

Frank nodded, already looking down at the accentuated thighs and private bulge.

Verneus slowly unfastened his trousers, peeled the yellow breeches down to his knees and over his feet, then removed them entirely.

Verneus stood still, his bare flesh exposed under the moonlight for Frank's eyes and curiosity. His cock hung thick and ample. Frank allowed himself the liberty of touching it all, working his way down from the chest to the well-endowed prick. He pressed on it, feeling its consistency, before stroking it tenderly.

Verneus tossed his head back in ecstasy, moaning and then grunting. To Frank's surprise, Verneus howled loudly, his voice blasting into the night. Frank's ears rang, but Verneus howled again, this time with a different and more surreal tone, as if he were a real animal and no longer human. Frank yanked his hand away, looking into Verneus's face. A set of fangs appeared to be growing from Verneus's cave-like mouth.

Frank took a step back as Verneus dropped to the floor, as if in pain.

Verneus's body coiled as he moaned. He extended his hands upward, curling his fingers as he looked up at Frank with wide eyes that glistened with certain apprehension.

To Frank's horror, Verneus began to transform. What had been a perfect human mouth morphed into a distortion. What had been a perfect face and body exploded in fur. His back became ribbed and narrow, while deformed bones began to burst from beneath his flesh, causing him to take the shape of an abominable creature.

Verneus howled again, this time even louder, as if to release his pain. He now looked more like an animal than any sort of man.

Frank rushed into the woods, his heart racing as if it might erupt from his chest. He ran toward the house, letting out a high-pitched wail. He could hear Verneus howl once again behind him.

The dark silhouette of the cottage came into view ahead. He was almost there, but the howl sounded closer. Foolishly, Frank looked back. His predator now resembled a large werewolf, thumping on all four legs, exposing its oversized fangs.

Frank trembled in utter fear, yelping as he continued running toward the safe haven. Behind him, he could hear the animal approaching, its paws pounding the forest floor. A grunting and snorting sound spewed from the animal's flaring nostrils.

"Help!" Frank screamed before storming into the house. Slamming the door shut behind him, he finally felt safe.

The two wax men looked up at him briefly before returning to their meal, as if undisturbed by Frank's hysterical commotion. The werewolf thumped on the door. Frank resumed screaming. It clawed at the doorframe viciously before its claws began gashing and penetrating the wood.

"Help!" Frank yelled at the men.

They smiled, exposing their long, white canine teeth.

Frank felt as though he would collapse in fear. "Help me, somebody!"

Backing away from the door, he watched the werewolf break through the wood and rush toward him. The beast clawed into Frank's chest, his blood splattering and gushing. With unstoppable rage, it continued to shred Frank's flesh, tearing off his legs, arms, and head.

The two men watched, laughing and snarling as if preparing to join the werewolf's feast. But they didn't. They began fighting the werewolf instead, perhaps in competition for the pieces of Frank's body. It took only seconds for the werewolf to latch onto the neck of one of the men, while the other continued to brawl, sinking his fangs into the werewolf's neck. But such punctures were harmless to the alpha werewolf. With only one strike, it tore through the other man's chest and proceeded to feast savagely on its new prey. The werewolf then stopped and looked up, proudly howling at the full moon.

Paul thought the sight was pretty grisly, with all the blood and flesh everywhere. The way the golden eyes of the werewolf reflected under the light, as if they were human—that creeped him out.

Paul continued to amble amongst the scenes until he noticed a pale figure, half smiling, with dark raven waves curling over its shoulders. From its black clothes, long cape, and white fangs, Paul figured it was a vampire. The figure was tall and its face was handsome, as Paul knew vampires were sometimes portrayed.

He didn't think the sculptor could have done a better job on the race, especially those brown eyes. They seemed to hypnotize Paul. He examined everything about the figure, including the way it stood—statuesque and illustrious.

He was so taken with the handsome face and mesmerizing eyes, he hadn't noticed the second figure crouching below the vampire's knees. It was a female, gripping the vampire's pants. She wore a short, silky, white negligee, and one of her breasts was exposed, thanks to the spaghetti strap having slid past her shoulder.

She appeared to be weeping, but not from fear. She seemed to be pleading, almost as if she didn't want the man at her side to leave. Her neck was marred by two small puncture wounds.

Paul brought his fingers up to his own neck. He wondered how it felt to be bitten by the vampire, but more than anything, he couldn't peel his eyes away from the vampire's eyes. They gazed into him, as if they had captured him fully.

Suddenly, they had.

Even as the vampire reached for Paul's hand, Paul wanted nothing more than to let him lead the way. The woman at his feet looked up at Paul and the vampire.

"It belongs to me!" she cried.

The vampire looked down with disdain. "Quiet!"

"No, this isn't fair!" She glared at Paul. "You bastard! You cannot take what is not yours! He is mine! Mine!"

Paul didn't answer. Instead, he followed the vampire from the room. When they stepped out of the small flat and into the desolate night streets, Paul noticed his clothes were different. His new trousers and blazer seemed to be from the late nineteenth century, just like the vampire's clothes.

The two of them stood in a cobblestone alley, walled in by tall, narrow buildings.

Paul could see the Eiffel Tower in the distance, until a carriage led by two black horses with long, feathered headdresses pulled up.

"Please, Paul. Be my guest," said the vampire, opening the carriage door for Paul.

Paul entered the small compartment, waiting for the vampire to sit at his side. He wasn't sure how the vampire had guessed his name, but he didn't care.

"I am Darius," he said. "And tonight, you are my guest."

"What about your pleading woman?" Paul asked.

"You mean Darla? I did not wish to make her my companion."

"I think she was expecting it."

Darius leaned his head against the dark, tufted leather so that the edge of his curved hair brushed it, resting at his shoulders. "One must learn to *not* depend on the abilities and strengths of others, especially when they have nothing to offer." He caressed the side of Paul's face with the back of his hand. "Darla has nothing to offer. You, Paul, have plenty to offer."

"Like what?"

"Companionship."

"Really?"

"Absolutely."

"Actually, I could offer anything but that." Paul let out a deep breath. "I've never been able to commit to anyone. And the times I did try, all I could think about was how to get out of it."

Darius grinned. "That's not what I saw in your eyes earlier. The eyes cannot lie."

Paul didn't respond. He attempted to remember how Darius's eyes had drawn him in, but how he got where he was didn't matter. All that mattered was to be next to Darius and accompany him on the dark night's ride.

Paul remained this way, silent and content to be at his side. Outside, the Parisian streets were desolate. Paul gazed at the lonely, narrow alleyways—until something distracted him. The horses snorted. They had come to a stop.

"We are here," said Darius.

Before Paul could say anything, the carriage door was opened by a young male attendant, who greeted Darius with familiarity. The young man reached for Paul's hand, helping him out of the carriage and then leading him toward their destination.

Paul followed Darius into a large bar filled with patrons. A woman in a black silk gown sang *a cappella* on the stage. The place was dim and elegant with somber colors. Most of the crowd sat at round tables, while others crowded along the edge of the bar. A female hostess in a French bustier roamed about the room, balancing a tray of wine goblets. Many lustful eyes watched Darius and Paul, in particular Paul.

"Welcome back, Mister Darius," said a lanky host dressed in black. His eyes were large and his face was as pale as Darius's. "We have your usual table for you, sir."

"Thank you, Pierre."

Pierre led them to a corner booth with only a small chandelier above them to reflect Darius's handsome features.

A server placed two silver chalices filled with red in front of Paul and Darius. Darius raised his glass, toasted Paul, then consumed its contents in one gulp.

Paul watched and drank. He tasted alcohol, perhaps wine, but also a mixture of something salty and almost flesh-like.

Darius winked and smiled. "It's my favorite drink. But I'm sure *you* taste even better."

Paul remained silent, moving only his eyes as he scoped the room. His sense of safety and comfort was dissolving. For the first time since meeting Darius, a fear was beginning to swell inside him.

In that moment, the female singer began a new song with a cello accompanying her. The combination was dismal and ethereal, as if the woman's lyrics, which Paul could not translate, yearned and ached for an old love.

Paul looked up, expecting to see the woman onstage, but instead became startled by the sudden figure standing between him and Darius. To his horror, it was Darla from the flat, and she wasn't alone.

"That's him!" Darla shouted to an entourage of mixed sexes behind her—a gang of people who had just barged in with her, all gnashing their fangs, as bitter and heated as Darla. They carried an arsenal of knives, wooden stakes, chains, and other weapons aimed in Paul and Darius's direction. Paul counted ten of them easy.

"He's the intruder!" Darla cried. "He's the one that convinced Darius to deprive me of what is mine! And now, Darius has deceived me and plans to share the Gift with him instead! They are breaking the law!"

Pierre shoved his commanding presence between Paul and the enraged crowd. "Please, I cannot have this mayhem in my place. You must all leave at once!"

"Mind your own business, or you'll get what's yours!" Darla shouted.

"Yes!" someone sympathized. "Let's kill the intruder!"

"Get them!" the woman insisted. "And now both of them will have to pay! Both of them!"

Within seconds, the crowd had swarmed the booth, yanking Paul out as they pulled his hair and placed a sharp knife under his neck. Darius vanished, reappearing in a split second, at the other end of the bar. His demeanor was calm and unrushed, even as he raised his arms and voice to the patrons at the bar. "Get them, everyone!"

Almost immediately, the rumble began amongst the dwellers of the night, some less powerful and less ancient than others. The elders had a clear advantage over the disobedient neophytes, including Darla, whose fury had initiated the battle.

One of the elders had wounded her brutally, but that did not stop her rage.

She charged Paul, aiming a wooden stake at his face, but Darius flew toward her and decapitated her with one blow.

The brawlers continued, knocking over a stray candle, which began to burn the bar. As the flames spread, screams filled the air. Paul started to run, heading for the door. He knew something was wrong and out of place. His heart pounded with fear. He could taste his own saliva, its mild thickness helping him to regain control of his senses. He remembered that somewhere, far away from the old, vampire-infested city of Paris, were two faithful friends. But where? Who were they exactly?

"Paul," someone whispered in his ear.

It was Darius.

Paul looked back at the chaos in the bar, the flames stirring heat and death. Amongst it all was that familiar face with the alluring eyes that had captured Paul powerfully, enticing him to succumb to the world of darkness.

They gazed at him keenly but seemed sad, as if Darius knew he had lost Paul already. If Paul wasn't mistaken, tears trickled down Darius's cheeks—tears of yearning, aching for Paul to remain at his side, just like Darla had pined for Darius.

This time the vampire's clothes were disheveled, his cape partially torn, while Paul's were still intact. Paul stood tall, as master to servant to the tortured and handsome vampire, who could escape and vanish if he were so inclined. But Darius stood in the middle of the chaos instead, gazing at Paul.

The vampire had exposed his passion and emotions without care. He wanted Paul and longed for him more than anyone ever had before. Paul knew nothing could stop Darius from detaining him if he so desired, and forcing him to remain at his side.

The words of the vampire ran through Paul's mind once more: "One must learn to *not* depend on the abilities and strengths of others."

Paul's eyes remained fixed on the tall and handsome figure with the long cape. Already, Paul's senses were becoming clearer—*an old home with friends.* That's when he knew. He knew precisely what he wanted. And with whom.

Paul walked toward Darius, who rapidly wrapped Paul in his arms and cape. Paul tilted his head, resting it against Darius's chest.

The breath came at him, brushing Paul's neck before coiling it and unleashing a pleasant warmth. Soon, he felt Darius's lips graze his neck and kiss it gently.

His fangs stabbed Paul's neck like two vicious needles. Out of the wounds came the taste of Paul—over and over—flowing unstoppably into Darius's mouth. Red pulsated with life until the rush waned, almost as quickly as it had begun.

Paul felt himself weaken more and more until darkness finally came. Whether he would return and awaken as something else, he did not know. He remained there under the comfort of the vampire, a figure concealed under Darius's black cape, dead perhaps.

As for Eric, he couldn't tell if the victim under the vampire's cape was a man or a woman. In reality, it didn't matter to Eric. He walked away, in search of Frank or Paul. He looked ahead, squinting at the aisles of figures.

"Frank?" His voice echoed inside the long room. The figures watched him in silence, some grinning, while others growled or mourned, pleading for mercy in the midst of insanity—lovers and enemies appearing fervently dismayed.

"Frank? Paul?" Eric called out. "Where are you guys?"

Suddenly, he could no longer enjoy the entertaining figures until he found Frank and Paul. He sped through the rows of wax beings until something caught his attention. This particular wax display was not of a human.

A gold and silver rhombus shined under the light. Large axles ran along the edge of what looked like an instrument panel, with controls, whirls, spindles, and digital displays—in particular, four large, glowing, neon-green numbers.

Eric smiled, studying the arrangement of the machine's gadgets. It almost looked like a real operating mechanism. Eric glanced around, as if to ensure no one was watching, before setting foot beyond the boundary of *his* world and another. He reached for the handle of the wax time machine's compartment. And to his astonishment, it opened.

Eric pressed his hands over the cold metal, which had been wax only seconds ago. As for the inside, more dials and levers appeared over a dashboard, facing a seat just waiting for him.

Eric beamed in fascination as he hunched forward, stepping inside the machine. His hands pressed on its interior walls and dashboard. Undoubtedly, the machines insides were more precise and efficient than he could have guessed. Eyes shining with wonder, he sat on the small, dark, leather seat. He was about to examine the dashboard more closely, when the door slammed shut, sealing him in darkness.

"Hey!" Eric shouted, pounding on the solid metal door.

To his amazement, the dashboard's lights, dials, and screens flashed and flared green, red, and yellow. Digital numbers and other data activated and flickered. The mock-up was no longer a counterfeit display but a genuine portal preparing to teleport Eric to a different dimension.

Eric continued to shout at the numbers in front of him as they whirled uncontrollably. Even Eric's pounding fists, against the door and dashboard, could not stop the heated time machine. In the midst of his pandemonium, he remembered the four digits on the outside of the machine's glass pane: the year 1938.

He looked up at the display, and to his horror, the numbers came to a halt at the same year. It lit up in red, flickering at him before all lights went off again, returning him to darkness— and silence. He banged on the door, which, to his surprise, opened instantly.

Eric froze. He scanned the floor and then the room as he set one foot outside, looking for recognizable objects.

No wax figures appeared anywhere.

He recognized the mansion's wax museum room, but all he saw was antique furniture.

"What the fuck!"

Eric stormed out of the room and down the familiar corridor with Oriental rugs, framed artwork, and shelved books. He nearly stumbled going downstairs, but nothing about the living room seemed changed.

He could see only one difference.

Actually, he could see only one person.

Eric recognized his eyes. The distinguished man before him was Gregorio, perhaps a young man in his late teens.

Either way, Eric didn't care. He shoved his way past and flung the door open. Los Angeles appeared before him, a small city that would one day become a dense metropolis.

Behind him, Gregorio called his name, invited him to stay, to be with him, so that the two could spend *time* together—countless *time*, where Gregorio was young and the city could age with them both.

About the Author

Julian Lopez is the author of the novel *Missed Connections* and of several short stories published in anthologies from Alyson Publications and Icarus. He has contributed articles to several magazines on interior architecture, lifestyle, and animal welfare and has served as editor for the *spcaLA* magazine. An LA native, Julian is a designer in commercial architecture who devotes his spare time to writing fiction, vintage hunting, and exploring LA with his dog, Fina.

Books Available from Bold Strokes Books

Cirque des Freaks and Other Tales of Horror by Julian Lopez. Explore the pleasure of horror in this compilation that delivers like the horror classics...good ole tales of terror. (978-1-63555-689-6)

Face the Music by Ali Vali. Sweet music is the last thing that happens when Nashville music producer Mason Liner, and daughter of country royalty Victoria Roddy are thrown together in an effort to save country star Sophie Roddy's career. (978-1-63555-532-5)

Flavor of the Month by Georgia Beers. What happens when baker Charlie and chef Emma realize their differing paths have led them right back to each other? (978-1-63555-616-2)

Mending Fences by Angie Williams. Rancher Bobbie Del Rey and veterinarian Grace Hammond are about to discover if heartbreaks of the past can ever truly be mended. (978-1-63555-708-4)

Silk and Leather: Lesbian Erotica with an Edge edited by Victoria Villasenor. This collection of stories by award winning authors offers fantasies as soft as silk and tough as leather. The only question is: How far will you go to make your deepest desires come true? (978-1-63555-587-5)

The Last Place You Look by Aurora Rey. Dumped by her wife and looking for anything but love, Julia Pierce retreats to her hometown, only to rediscover high school friend Taylor Winslow, who's secretly crushed on her for years. (978-1-63555-574-5)

The Mortician's Daughter by Nan Higgins. A singer on the verge of stardom discovers she must give up her dreams to live a life in service to ghosts. (978-1-63555-594-3)

The Real Thing by Laney Webber. When passion flares between actress Virginia Green and masseuse Allison McDonald, can they be sure it's the real thing? (978-1-63555-478-6)

What the Heart Remembers Most by M. Ullrich. For college sweethearts Jax Levine and Gretchen Mills could an accident be the second chance neither knew they wanted? (978-1-63555-401-4)

White Horse Point by Andrews & Austin. Mystery writer Taylor James finds herself falling for the mysterious woman on White Horse Point who lives alone, protecting a secret she can't share about a murderer who walks among them. (978-1-63555-695-7)

Femme Tales by Anne Shade. Six women find themselves in their own real-life fairy tales when true love finds them in the most unexpected ways. (978-1-63555-657-5)

Jellicle Girl by Stevie Mikayne. One dark summer night, Beth and Jackie go out to the canoe dock. Two years later, Beth is still carrying the weight of what happened to Jackie. (978-1-63555-691-9)

Le Berceau by Julius Eks. If only Ben could tear his heart in two, then he wouldn't have to choose between the love of his life and the most beautiful boy he has ever seen. (978-1-63555-688-9)

My Date with a Wendigo by Genevieve McCluer. Elizabeth Rosseau finds her long lost love and the secret community of fiends she's now a part of. (978-1-63555-679-7)

On the Run by Charlotte Greene. Even when they're cute blondes, it's stupid to pick up hitchhikers, especially when they've just broken out of prison, but doing so is about to change Gwen's life forever. (978-1-63555-682-7)

Perfect Timing by Dena Blake. The choice between love and family has never been so difficult, and Lynn's and Maggie's different visions of the future may end their romance before it's begun. (978-1-63555-466-3)

The Mail Order Bride by R Kent. When a mail order bride is thrust on Austin, he must choose between the bride he never wanted or the dream he lives for. (978-1-63555-678-0)

Through Love's Eyes by C.A. Popovich. When fate reunites Brittany Yardin and Amy Jansons, can they move beyond the pain of their past to find love? (978-1-63555-629-2)

To the Moon and Back by Melissa Brayden. Film actress Carly Daniel thinks that stage work is boring and unexciting, but when she accepts a lead role in a new play, stage manager Lauren Prescott tests both her heart and her ability to share the limelight. (978-1-63555-618-6)

Tokyo Love by Diana Jean. When Kathleen Schmitt is given the opportunity to be on the cutting edge of AI technology, she never thought a failed robotic love companion would bring her closer to her neighbor, Yuriko Velucci, and finding love in unexpected places. (978-1-63555-681-0)

Brooklyn Summer by Maggie Cummings. When opposites attract, can a summer of passion and adventure lead to a lifetime of love? (978-1-63555-578-3)

City Kitty and Country Mouse by Alyssa Linn Palmer. Pulled in two different directions, can a city kitty and country mouse fall in love and make it work? (978-1-63555-553-0)

Elimination by Jackie D. When a dangerous homegrown terrorist seeks refuge with the Russian mafia, the team will be put to the ultimate test. (978-1-63555-570-7)

In the Shadow of Darkness by Nicole Stiling. Angeline Vallencourt is a reluctant vampire who must decide what she wants more—obscurity, revenge, or the woman who makes her feel alive. (978-1-63555-624-7)

On Second Thought by C. Spencer. Madisen is falling hard for Rae. Even single life and co-parenting are beginning to click. At least, that is, until her ex-wife begins to have second thoughts. (978-1-63555-415-1)

Out of Practice by Carsen Taite. When attorney Abby Keane discovers the wedding blogger tormenting her client is the woman she had a passionate, anonymous vacation fling with, sparks and subpoenas fly. Legal Affairs: one law firm, three best friends, three chances to fall in love. (978-1-63555-359-8)

Providence by Leigh Hays. With every click of the shutter, photographer Rebekiah Kearns finds it harder and harder to keep Lindsey Blackwell in focus without getting too close. (978-1-63555-620-9)

Taking a Shot at Love by KC Richardson. When academic and athletic worlds collide, will English professor Celeste Bouchard and basketball coach Lisa Tobias ignore their attraction to achieve their professional goals? (978-1-63555-549-3)

Flight to the Horizon by Julie Tizard. Airline captain Kerri Sullivan and flight attendant Janine Case struggle to survive an emergency water landing and overcome dark secrets to give love a chance to fly. (978-1-63555-331-4)

In Helen's Hands by Nanisi Barrett D'Arnuk. As her mistress, Helen pushes Mickey to her sensual limits, delivering the pleasure only a BDSM lifestyle can provide her. (978-1-63555-639-1)

Jamis Bachman, Ghost Hunter by Jen Jensen. In Sage Creek, Utah, a poltergeist stirs to life and past secrets emerge. (978-1-63555-605-6)

Moon Shadow by Suzie Clarke. Add betrayal, season with survival, then serve revenge smokin' hot with a sharp knife. (978-1-63555-584-4)

Spellbound by Jean Copeland and Jackie D. When the supernatural worlds of good and evil face off, love might be what saves them all. (978-1-63555-564-6)

Temptation by Kris Bryant. Can experienced nanny Cassie Miller deny her growing attraction and keep her relationship with her boss professional? Or will they sidestep propriety and give in to temptation? (978-1-63555-508-0)

The Inheritance by Ali Vali. Family ties bring Tucker Delacroix and Willow Vernon together, but they could also tear them, and any chance they have at love, apart. (978-1-63555-303-1)

Thief of the Heart by MJ Williamz. Kit Hanson makes a living seducing rich women in casinos and relieving them of the expensive jewelry most won't even miss. But her streak ends when she meets beautiful FBI agent Savannah Brown. (978-1-63555-572-1)

Date Night by Raven Sky. Quinn and Riley are celebrating their one-year anniversary. Such an important milestone is bound to result in some extraordinary sexual adventures, but precisely how extraordinary is up to you, dear reader. (978-1-63555-655-1)

Face Off by PJ Trebelhorn. Hockey player Savannah Wells rarely spends more than a night with any one woman, but when photographer Madison Scott buys the house next door, she's forced to rethink what she expects out of life. (978-1-63555-480-9)

Hot Ice by Aurora Rey, Elle Spencer, Erin Zak. Can falling in love melt the hearts of the iciest ice queens? Join Aurora Rey, Elle Spencer, and Erin Zak to find out! (978-1-63555-513-4)

Line of Duty by VK Powell. Dr. Dylan Carlyle's professional and personal life is turned upside down when a tragic event at Fairview Station pits her against ambitious, handsome police officer Finley Masters. (978-1-63555-486-1)

London Undone by Nan Higgins. London Craft reinvents her life after reading a childhood letter to her future self and in doing so finds the love she truly wants. (978-1-63555-562-2)

Lunar Eclipse by Gun Brooke. Moon De Cruz lives alone on an uninhabited planet after being shipwrecked in space. Her life changes forever when Captain Beaux Lestarion's arrival threatens the planet and Moon's freedom. (978-1-63555-460-1)

One Small Step by Michelle Binfield. Iris and Cam discover the meaning of taking chances and following your heart, even if it means getting hurt. (978-1-63555-596-7)

Shadows of a Dream by Nicole Disney. Rainn has the talent to take her rock band all the way, but falling in love is a powerful distraction, and her new girlfriend's meth addiction might just take them both down. (978-1-63555-598-1)

Someone to Love by Jenny Frame. When Davina Trent is given an unexpected family, can she let nanny Wendy Darling teach her to open her heart to the children and to Wendy? (978-1-63555-468-7)

Tinsel by Kris Bryant. Did a sweet kitten show up to help Jessica Raymond and Taylor Mitchell find each other? Or is the holiday spirit to blame for their special connection? (978-1-63555-641-4)

Uncharted by Robyn Nyx. As Rayne Marcellus and Chase Stinsen track the legendary Golden Trinity, they must learn to put their differences aside and depend on one another to survive. (978-1-63555-325-3)

Where We Are by Annie McDonald. Can two women discover a way to walk on the same path together and discover the gift of staying in one spot, in time, in space, and in love? (978-1-63555-581-3)

A Moment in Time by Lisa Moreau. A longstanding family feud separates two women who unexpectedly fall in love at an antique clock shop in a small Louisiana town. (978-1-63555-419-9)